Follow Me

ANNIE SEATON

978-0-6483990-6-3

Dedication

This book is dedicated to our three beautiful grandchildren: Benny, Charlotte and Charlie.

Acknowledgments

Susanne Bellamy, and Roby Aiken, the best editors and proof readers ever!

.

PROLOGUE

David Morgan was sitting on Tony and Kathy's deck overlooking the sparkling waters of Sydney harbour. Megan had come back to Australia to pack up and head home with him.

Home—to his island in the Bahamas but he had promised her regular trips down under to visit the new baby sleeping in the pram beside Kathy.

'So where's the wedding going to be held?' Kathy asked as she leaned into the pram and picked up baby Jack.

Megan looked at her sister with a smile. 'David has offered to fly you all to his island. We were thinking of a Christmas wedding in the Bahamas.'

Tony nodded. 'As long as little Jack here is up to a long flight, that sounds fabulous.'

Megan jumped up as the doorbell rang. 'Beth's here!' David watched as she hurried inside to answer the door.

A young woman with long blonde hair had her arm through Megan's when she reappeared. They were both smiling as Megan led her friend across to the table.

'Beth, this is David.'

David stood and held out his hand. 'Hello, Beth. It's good to finally meet you.'

'You too,' Beth replied. 'I've heard so much about you from Megan. And Megan said that you met my Aunt Alice briefly before she passed away.'

'I did. She was a sweet old lady.' David swallowed. It still made him nervous, wondering if his dual life would ever be discovered. The further he and Megan were from the stones in Glastonbury, the happier he was.

'I never met her, but my mother remembers her as a bit of an old hippie.'

David simply smiled.

Beth put her head to the side and looked at him curiously. 'Did you ever meet her husband? Or did she talk about him?

'No.' David swallowed again, unsure of how much more to say. 'I didn't. I always thought she hadn't married.'

'I thought she had from what Mum said, but I'm probably wrong, but I'll know soon.' Beth turned back to Megan, excitement in her voice. 'I have news.'

Excitement bobbled in Beth's voice and Megan smiled at her. 'It looks like you've won the lottery.'

'Better than that! I'm going to England to live in Aunt Alice's cottage for a few months.'

David and Megan looked at each other. 'That's…um, exciting,' Megan said. 'But what on earth are you going to do in a cottage way out in the country for a few months? There's not a lot there, just a small village.'

'Mum found a trunk when we were over there ten years ago and it was full of Aunt Alice's journals. I read a couple when we were over there.'

'Journals?' Megan's voice was so soft, David barely heard her question. 'What sort of journals?'

He stood still as he waited for Beth to answer.

'Her life,' she said with a smile. 'An amazing resource. A personal diary from the second World War forward. I'm thinking about writing a book.'

David and Megan looked at each other.

'A personal diary?' Megan said as trepidation settled in David's chest.

Bloody hell, what had Alice recorded?

Chapter 1

As the jet had crossed the English Channel the land appeared below, and Beth McLaren stared down at the patchwork of fields. A frisson of excitement unfurled in her chest. The plane descended and the houses and buildings of London spread out beneath her. It was hard to contain the anticipation that was coursing through her as she'd hurried to the train station at Heathrow.

Now at Paddington station, the announcement of the train's imminent arrival crackled over the loudspeaker. The robotic voice was hard to hear, and Beth tilted her head as there was a lull in the noise from the crowd jammed in the station. A constant stream of commuters pushed past her, heads down and clutching briefcases, backpacks or suitcases. Children in a group nearby squealed as the announcement was made and a baby in a pram behind her screamed at full volume.

The winter afternoon chill had settled in, but Beth didn't care about the weather. Nothing could bring her euphoric mood down: cold, noise or tiredness from the long haul flight. She'd been so busy making plans in her head, and thinking about the cottage she'd had little sleep after they'd taken off from Singapore. As she'd stepped off the plane at Heathrow, gone through passport control and looked for the directions to the airport station, she'd quivered with excitement. She was here finally after years of dreaming, and no matter what opposition she'd faced, she was here to stay.

The strangest sense of homecoming engulfed her; she knew it was where she belonged, as Another group of school children chattered beside her in French, but she barely paid them any attention as her spirits lifted even higher. No matter what everyone had said, this was her plan, her decision and her way of coping with what life had thrown at her.

Beth bit her lip and held back the anticipation that was coursing through her. The feeling had taken root as she'd waited for her flight in Sydney, and had stayed with her the whole long trip. Months and months of planning, hours of reading, and research had brought her to this moment, and she had to pinch herself to believe it was actually happening.

God knew, she'd daydreamed about this constantly since she was eighteen-years-old.

'I can't believe you're going to throw away all that hard work you've done at the university.' Mum had shaken her head as they'd sat in the coffee lounge at the international airport. 'Your father is furious that you knocked back the offer of working with Dr Hendricks. And why you resigned! Surely you could have taken leave, Beth?'

'Mum, I am twenty-nine-years old. What I choose to do with my life, and my career, has nothing to do with Dad—' she cleared her throat—'or anyone but me. Is that why he didn't come to see me off?'

'No. I believe he had another appointment.'

Beth tried not to let the hurt of being relegated to appointment status with her father hurt too much. At least her mother had made the effort to come to the airport, even if it was to talk her out of going at the last minute.

'You're going to England simply because of some romanticised notion of what you think you read in an old diary when you were a child. I've never heard anything so ridiculous in my life.'

'I wasn't a child. Give me credit for some intelligence.' Beth folded her arms and turned to look at the flight board. 'I have to go soon, so please let's not argue, Mum.'

She may as well not have spoken.

'And you're a historian. Your future at the university is so bright. Darling, please, please, think this through again. It's not too late. You can't just quit a job that pays so much and brings so much prestige.'

'I have David and Megan's wedding in Scotland. If it had been in the Bahamas I would have gone there, so the change of venue gives me the opportunity to do two things that are important to me. And no matter where it's held I wouldn't miss Megan's wedding for the world.'

Disappointment at the lack of support from her parents threatened to take the gloss off her adventure. 'I have to go now, Mum.'

'But what about Ph—'

Beth put her hand up. 'Don't go there, please.' Thankfully it was time to go through security before her mother could bring up what they both knew was the issue not to be raised.

The elephant in the room.

The elephant in my life.

Until she could put that fiasco behind her and establish some sort of stability in her emotions—and create her new life—her self-confidence had taken a beating.

Mum didn't know the full story, and as far as Beth was concerned, she never would. No one would. Private humiliation that kept her awake at nights, but if her parents knew the truth, and tried to offer tea and sympathy, Beth knew she wouldn't be able to cope with their concern.

Or more likely in recent months, gin and sympathy if her mother had anything to do with it. Since her parents had separated—when Dad found himself a later model woman—Mum had been drinking way too much.

She refused to let the attitude of her parents, and past events impact on her anticipation. This, was her third trip to England where in two short visits, Beth had felt more at home than she did in suburban Sydney where she'd been born and grown up.

Her first visit overseas —and to the cottage— had been when her father had had a work trip over to the UK, and he had taken all of the family with him. Beth—at nine—had been more interested in going to Euro Disney Resort near Paris, along with her older brother, Joshua than the cottage and an ancient aunt. They had barely taken notice of the tall woman with the long grey braids who lived in the cottage in the south of England they had visited briefly. All she could remember from that visit was the yellow roses that covered the cottage and the huge bees buzzing around in the sunlight. And the unusual perfume that her mum's aunt had worn.

'Patchouli!' Mum had sniffed disparagingly when they'd driven off in the hire car. 'She's a relic of the hippie seventies, that's for sure.'

The second visit her family had paid to the cottage had been the year after Great-Aunt Alice had passed. That had been over ten years ago, when Beth had been in her late teens.

They'd gone over to sort out the will and the estate. Beth had taken a few months off between school and university to accompany them on this trip. Her place in the nursing degree had been confirmed. Josh had been at university already and hadn't come with them. It had been a very different visit to the one with the memories of the roses. Mid-winter, cold and bleak , the weather had matched the sombre mood. Mum and Dad had been barely speaking; Beth later learned that the trip was one to try to repair the rift in their marriage.

They hadn't arrived in time for the November funeral; a friend of her great aunt had organised the formalities. Beth had been pleased when her mother had decided not to sell the cottage, but to let it out, thus necessitating the huge—and hurried— clean out.

She'd helped her parents clean out cupboards, wardrobes and garden sheds.

'Royden?' Mum called. 'Come and help me please.'

Beth had looked up from the kitchen sink where she'd been sorting out crockery so they could leave a decent set for future tenants. It had been a slow, but interesting, task; some of the pieces that Alice had collected over her lifetime were quite valuable. Shelley tea cups and Maling plates, sets of Crown Devon and the odd Coalport vase, thrown in with cheap and chipped op shop crockery, had her shaking her head as she kept a close eye on the imprints on the base of each piece.

'You're going to have to get some of this valued,' she called out to her mother.

'I'll have a look later.' Mum was kneeling at a low door set in the wall next to the dresser. It was painted the same bright yellow as the kitchen walls and was hidden in a dark corner away from the window. A small circular handle, in the same yellow, was on the top of the door.

She pulled it open as Beth watched, and her mother's voice was muffled as she put her head into the space.

'It's a cellar and it's absolutely chockers with wine.'

'Now I like the sound of that,' Dad said rubbing his hands together. 'A drink might warm us up.'

The cottage was cold and although the flames crackled merrily in the fireplace in the small sitting room, you had to stand in front of it to feel any warmth.

Beth pulled the rubber gloves from her hands and walked across the room. She loved this cottage, the low ceilings, the curved staircase up to the tiny bedrooms and bathroom; the flower-patterned sofas and the mullioned windows filled the cottage with character. If she closed her eyes, Beth could imagine that it had been just the same a couple of hundred years ago. The atmosphere was heavy with history.

Dad had followed Mum through the narrow doorway, and Beth wasn't far behind him. She could hear the groan that Dad emitted.

'God, I thought we were almost done, but look at all these bloody trunks.' He turned to Beth. 'Give us a hand, please. I'll lift them to the door, there's a couple of steps in here, and then you can slide them out.' He lifted the first one and carried it across to the small doorway. 'Not too heavy. One, two, three . . .four more to come.'

Beth slid the trunks one by one along the flagged stones on the kitchen floor and across the faded rose-patterned carpet floor in the sitting room.

'There's one more at the back here.' Mum's voice was faint.

Beth crossed back to the kitchen, and looked out into the garden at the back while she waited for the next trunk. The sky was heavy and she was desperately hoping it would snow before they left tomorrow. A small red-breasted bird sat on the window sill pecking at the crumbs she'd left out there after breakfast.

'Bloody heck, this feels like it's full of bricks.' Dad's eyes narrowed as he came out of the cellar. 'Could be the missing bloke.'

'Royden.' Mum's lips pursed in a warning as Beth turned to them.

'Who's missing?' she asked. 'What bloke?'

'No one. Your father's being his usual silly self.' Her mother spoke brightly, but Beth caught the tight glance she directed at her husband. 'What was in the others, Beth?

She shook her head. 'I don't know. Let's have a look.'

Dad carried the last trunk across with exaggerated huffing, and put it on the floor next to the others. 'Waste of time if you ask me. Just add them to the pile for the rubbish tip.'

'No one asked you, Royden, and Alice was my aunt, so it has nothing to do with you.'

Beth leaned forward and flipped open the lock at the front of the smallest. 'Oh, look. It's full of shoes.' She lifted a pair out and stared at them. 'How old are these?'

They were made of soft fawn leather, and the laces wound around the sole, in an unusual way she'd never seen before. 'They're so soft. I wonder if they'll fit.' She took off the thick woolly socks she'd had on to keep her feet warm and slipped them both on and looked down at her feet.

'Perfect fit. They're gorgeous.'

Mum threw her a distracted glance. 'Yes, they're pretty. Is there anything else of interest in that trunk?'

'No, just about a dozen pairs of shoes. They're all so different to anything I've seen. Maybe they're from a historical display or something.' She looked up at her mother and was surprised to see a wary expression quickly masked. 'Didn't Great-Aunt Alice have something to do with a historical society or something, I remember you talking about her love of history once Mum?'

Her mother waved a dismissive hand. 'I can't remember. Now hurry up we've got a lot to get through.'

The other three small trunks held clothing, and Beth was fascinated by what was in there. She held up a white linen petticoat. 'This has to be part of a collection. Look at the stitching on it, it's really old.'

'I'll organise for someone to come in and have a look. And at the china too. I heard you ask when I was in the cellar.' Her mother turned to Dad. 'Royden, I think we're going to have to delay our return trip. Some of this stuff might be valuable.'

Dad shook his head. 'No. We can't I've got too much on to stay any longer. Besides it's a few old clothes and shoes and some old cups. How valuable can it be? No. We're still leaving tomorrow.'

'What's in the heavy one, Mum?' Beth wandered over, ignoring the argument that her parents were involved in. As their voices rose, her mother gestured to the kitchen, and they walked out, leaving Beth to open the final trunk. It was more substantial than the others had been, and the leather lid was embossed. As Beth ran her fingers over the pattern, she noticed that amongst the leaf pattern, a set of initials were entwined. A fancy A and M in an antique style font was interlaced with a B and V. She peered down at it, her fingers caressing the soft leather. The back door closed and then there was no sound of their voices.

She undid the latches, and the leather creaked as the lid lifted. The familiar—and one of Beth's favourite—smells wafted up. Old books. Leather and old paper. Her eyes widened as she looked at four rows of book spines in neat rows. A collection of old books filled the trunk. She reached in and lifted a book from the end and realised why the trunk had been so heavy. The books were double stacked. There was another layer of books below the top rows.

Carrying the book she'd picked up over to the sofa next to the fire, she settled into the cushions warm from the fire. Beth went to stretch her feet out to the fire and realised she was still wearing the old leather shoes. As she slipped them off and toasted her bare feet in front of the warmth, the back door opened.

'Where are you, Beth?' Mum called from the kitchen.

'In front of the fire. The last trunk was full of old books.'

Dad walked in, rubbing his hands together. 'Bloody hell, it's cold out there. Your mother's worried about the value of some of this stuff, so we're going to take the good stuff up to the small bedroom, and leave it for a valuer. Whatever they sell, they can send us a cheque.' He leaned over the chair and looked at the book that Beth held.

'What have you got there?' Mum came into the room and sniffed as she looked at the open trunk.

'I don't know.' Beth turned the yellow pages carefully. Spidery handwriting filled the pages, and she reached over and switched on the lamp on the small table beside the chair. 'It looks like a diary, or maybe a handwritten story.' She peered down at the writing but it was hard to decipher. 'I don't think it is Aunt Alice's. It looks way too old for that.'

'Oh, it'll be hers. Drove her family crazy when she was a kid, your grandmother used to tell me. Alice was always scribbling. Letters, stories, diaries. They won't be worth anything .' Another dismissive wave as she reached down and took the book from Beth. 'Yes, it's her writing. Your grandmother and I had enough letters from Alice over the years for me to recognise it.' She flicked through the book and then put it back in the trunk. 'They can probably go with the rubbish. Come on, there's still a lot to do upstairs.'

'You can't throw them out!' Beth jumped to her feet and put her hands on her hips. 'There's so much history in there. I'll take them home with us.'

Dad shook his head. 'And just how do you plan on doing that? We'll have enough excess luggage without this pile of old books. We'll burn them out the back.'

'No!' Beth turned to her mother for support. 'Mum, you can't burn them. Please.'

The look that her mother gave her husband was calculating and Beth bit back a sigh. It might be a mean way to get her own way, but if Dad said one thing, Mum would always go the opposite way.

'All right, we'll put them back in the trunk and store them in the cellar. I'm going to put a few things in there and we'll lock the door. One day we'll come back.'

##

Mum hadn't been able to understand her fascination with the old books as they'd moved upstairs to sort out the clothes and possessions in the two small bedrooms.

'It would make it a lot quicker if you'd come upstairs and help us sort out the junk up here, instead of sitting down there, reading the ramblings of an old woman. Aunt Alice was off with the pixies most of her life.'

'I do remember the one time she came to visit us in Sydney,' Beth said softly as she put the book aside and followed her mother up the narrow wooden staircase. 'She told the best stories. I still remember how she used to tell me about the fairies

16

in the garden. I looked for them for a long time after she left.'

'Well, we've only got one more night here before we go to London, and there's still the bedrooms and attic to go through.

'Was Great Aunt Alice a historian?' she asked her mother as they lifted a candlewick bedspread off the single bed in the last room. The fabric was threadbare, and it came apart on one side as they lifted in.

'That one can go in the bin,' her mother said. 'Why do you ask?' Her eyes dropped to the ornaments on the old dresser and Beth sensed that she didn't want to meet her gaze.

'Oh, just what I flicked through in that first book. The diaries are almost like a history of the area from medieval times.' Her eyes were wide as she finally caught her mother's eyes. 'It's almost a novel the way she writes it. It brings history to life. Can I take one home?'

Her mother's face closed and she shook her head. 'No. Whatever they are they, belong here.

'I couldn't be bothered firing up that old Aga,' Mum said as they carried the last bag of rubbish out to the shed in the back garden three hours later. 'Let's go and get a drink.'

'Village pub for me too,' Dad said. 'I could go a pint after all the dust today.'

'I couldn't be bothered going out in the cold. I'll stay in and have some toast.' Beth was itching to look at the rest of the diaries before they went back into the cellar.

As her parents disappeared into the cold and dark to walk into the village, she headed for the kitchen. She looked around with pleasure. They'd left the small bibs and bobs on the window sill. Each of them seemed to be a souvenir of Great-Aunt Alice's travels. She let out a happy sigh; after she finished her degree she would back here to the cottage.

Beth cooked some toast, found a tin of sardines, made a pot of tea, and carried her light meal into the sitting room. She put the last log on the fire and settled back to read the diary she'd left out on the sofa.

Chapter 2

September 23rd.

The last of summer has passed, and I can't believe that I am still here. I arrived in the spring and I must leave in the autumn. I have to leave before the cold and the shorter days set in.

Keats Ode to Autumn is going round and round in my thoughts. I laughed. How wonderful would it be to visit the Lakes in the time of the Romantic poets.

This afternoon we lay under the spreading beech tree down the hill from the watermill, I lay there with my head in Branton's lap reciting my favourite poem.

'While barred clouds bloom the soft-dying day,
And touch the stubble-plains with rosy hue;
 Then in a wailful choir the small gnats mourn.'

'That's beautiful,' he said as his fingers played with my hair. Every so often he would lean forward and brush his lips across my cheek. A delicious shiver would run down my back as blue eyes with the long fringing black lashes held mine, sharing secrets that no one else could know.

If I record my days here, I will have those memories to revisit. But memories are cold comfort when you are alone.

The wheat harvest is finished; Branton has provided food and drink for the villagers for the past four days.

From sunrise until dark, the whole village has pitched in—men , women and children. The women and the children stayed out on the fields tying the wheat into sheaves to dry. When the field was full of sheaves of wheat, one of the children would run to the farm and tell old Billy Barnstaple to come. It was his job to bring the oxen-pulled cart into the field and load the sheaves until they were so high, some inevitably toppled over. It became a game for the children as they ran along next to the cart, and their laughter filled the air.

It made me smile and I was able to dispel my worry for a while.

Branton told me I must stay for the harvest festival, but I know I can't. If I dally too much longer it will be too hard to leave.

It could be impossible.

Would I care?

In one way, no, I wouldn't—but it would be irresponsible, and it will hurt my family. It's not the life for me, and it's not the right thing to do. It could change too many things, and that is something that I don't understand.

Maybe one day I will.

Maybe I can come back.

I know Branton doesn't want me to go, and if I am honest I could stay happily here for the rest of my life. He doesn't understand, because I cannot tell him why I must leave.

Despite the work of the harvest, and our weariness, each night we have been late going up to his rooms, and he has used all sorts of persuasions to convince me to stay. I won't write them here, as it would make any reader of my words blush. Those moments between us are private, and I will cherish them for as long as I live.

But the memories are in my head, and lodged in my heart and my soul. And no matter where I am, I will never forget these months. The thought of leaving him is breaking my heart, but I have to go. I can't stay with him.

But I can't take the risk of staying too long.

Or can I?

I love him and I am unsure if I will be able to go through with it.

Time is fleeting. Seize each opportunity. Make the most of every minute.

Chapter 3

They'd gone to London after the cottage had been sorted, stayed at a flash hotel and experienced a white Christmas. Beth hadn't read any more of the journals that trip; the time had passed too quickly; she'd seen the Tower of London and taken the train to Hampton Court, and visited the British Museum.

'We're going to Harrods tomorrow, Beth,' Mum had said the day before they were due to fly home but to her mother's disappointment Beth had shaken her head.

'I'm going to the British Museum, Mum. I'm not interested in the shops.'

Mum had been cross, but she'd still bought her a souvenir, and they'd headed home to Australia.

Before Beth knew it she was at university immersed in lectures and study, and loving it. She'd packed the journal she'd been reading and taken it back home with her. Visiting England, her great-aunt's cottage, and the diary had changed the direction of her life. On their return to Sydney— much to the surprise and disapproval of her parents—she had gone to the university and changed her course selection from nursing to history.

Mum's face had been a picture. 'But what about nursing? What on earth are you going to do with a history degree?' Her nose had wrinkled as disdain crossed her face. 'All you can do with that is teach. Surely not, Beth?'

Beth couldn't explain why she had felt the need to change. It was hard to understand herself; she just knew she had to do it.

'Yes, a history degree.' Her voice was firm as she held Mum's gaze. Worry filled her as she'd seen the dark shadows under her mother's eyes, and the shaking hand as she reached up to pat her hair in place.

'Your father is going to be very unhappy. He didn't pay all those private school fees so you could be a teacher!'

'I don't know what I'll do with it yet, Mum. I want to study history.'

Mum's impatient clicking of her tongue had more to do with the deterioration of her marriage than any worry about Beth's pattern of study.

Within three months Dad had moved out, and Beth tried to focus on her studies. The one journal she'd brought back from the cottage stayed in her thoughts.

Was the journal a diary? Or was it fiction?

But no matter how many new experiences she'd had that holiday in the city of London, she'd vowed to come back to the cottage in Somerset as soon as she'd finished her degree.

##

'And then life intruded' she muttered under her breath as she stood on the platform more than ten years later, waiting for the train that would take her to the cottage she'd longed to return to.

The words she'd read over and over had touched her. She craved more, and it became an obsession. In her waking thoughts and in her dreams, Beth had visualised the wonderful scenes that the words had conjured up.

This afternoon we lay under the spreading beech tree down the hill from the watermill, I lay there with my head in Branton's lap reciting my favourite poem.

She had gone to the university library and devoured every Thomas Hardy novel she could find. She'd immersed herself in the poetry of Wordsworth, Keats, Byron, Shelley, Blake and Coleridge.

Who had written the beautiful description of the medieval harvest, the lovers beneath the old beech tree and why had Aunt Alice transcribed it into her journal?

Perhaps there were more family history records somewhere? Maybe Alice had found them in the

British Library or in records at the local rectory. Beth's skills had developed as she completed her history degree, and then an honours year, and eventually taken up a tutoring position at the university.

Mum continued to worry about her interest in the journals and the cottage 'Beth, most girls go through a Mills and Boon stage of romance and then go out with real men. You have to forget those journals.'

The years had passed quickly, but Beth had never forgotten the rest of the journals stored in the cellar in the cottage in the south of England. Her best friend, Megan, travelled over to Somerset last year as part of her PhD research and stayed in the cottage. When Megan had visited, Beth didn't mention the journals stored away; she had a sense of ownership and didn't want to share them. Unexpectedly Megan had met and fallen in love with musician, David Morgan. When Megan had brought back photos of the cottage after her visit, Beth's desire—or her need— to visit had strengthened.

The incidents of the previous months had firmed her resolve and when the invitation to Megan and David's wedding—no longer to be held in the Bahamas, but now in a Scottish castle—had arrived, Beth had booked a one-way ticket to England.

So much for Mum's idea of romance and real men. After the last couple of years, Beth didn't believe in romance.

Now here she was standing on the platform at Paddington station, about to catch the train down to Castle Cary, and then it was a twenty-minute taxi ride to the cottage. She would spend three nights there before travelling up to Scotland for the wedding. David was organizing the transport.

'*Just be ready to be collected*,' Megan had written. '*You'll be picked up on the twenty-seventh Just pack a gorgeous dress, and something warm. Really, really warm.*

Rothmore Castle is cold!'

Beth smiled. She was looking forward to the wedding; it wasn't every day you got to go to a celebrity wedding in a Scottish castle. But first, she had three days to pull out the trunk holding the journals, snuggle on the sofa in front of the fire and immerse herself in reading.

Maybe she was going to be disappointed; Beth knew she was a very different person to the young girl who'd curled up in the same sofa, reading of harvest festivals, winnowing and true love. But she'd never forgotten that story she'd read in Alice's journal. And the other experiences that had formed a chronicle of her great aunt's life—or her imagination.

Beth was a woman now—and a woman who had learned her own hard lesson in life. Over the years as she had matured, she'd let the bleached blonde summer hair grow out, and had learned to accept her red hair and freckles. Years of trying to look like a beach girl on the northern beaches of Sydney were behind her. Now her long auburn hair was more often than not tidily secured with a butterfly clip in a roll at the back of her head. Her square tortoiseshell glasses completed the look of a serious academic.

Beth firmly believed she would never be classed as beautiful. Her nose was too long, and her eyes were too widely spaced. Her hair was pretty enough but it was a nuisance to leave it loose. The more she became immersed in her studies, the more, she had hidden behind what she accepted was a plain exterior.

Maybe if she'd taken more care with her appearance, things would have turned out differently. Maybe she would have taken more care in forming relationships. Maybe Phillip Steadman would never have destroyed her self-esteem.

The train trip through the rolling countryside to the small town of Castle Cary passed quickly, and soon Beth was lifting her suitcase and backpack onto the platform. The weather had closed in, and even though it was only mid-afternoon, it wouldn't be long before dark. She'd forgotten how early dusk fell in the English autumn, and she hurried out to the taxi rank that she remembered was outside the station.

She was in luck. Two empty taxis waited for passengers from the train, and she walked over to the first one.

'Hello, love. Where're you off to?' The taxi driver hurried around to help her with her bag.

'Violet Cottage.' She handed over her backpack, and put her handbag over her shoulder. 'It's halfway between Pilton and Glastonbury.'

He nodded. 'Aye. I know where it is. Jump in, it's about twenty minutes away.'

Despite the fading light, Beth's eyes were wide when the driver turned off A371 and drove down winding country lanes with hedgerows along the side. A couple of times he had to back up to let a tractor pass and he looked back apologetically. 'It's much quicker this way than to go along the main road and through Pilton.

Beth smiled and sat back. 'I'm enjoying the drive.' The last shards of sunlight shone through a gap in the hedge and Beth smiled as a couple of small birds hung upside down, pecking at the brush.

'Australian?' he asked.

Beth nodded. 'Yes. I've only just arrived.'

'We get a lot of Aussies here for the music festival in the summer, but not so many this time of the year.' His smile was wide as he made conversation, but Beth didn't mind. 'Visiting or on holidays, luv?'

'No, I'm here for a while. I'm going to be working here.'

He nodded and slowed the taxi as another tractor approached.

Beth had decided to use the journals to write a historical novel; her knowledge of medieval history and the stories in Alice's journal gave her a solid base to work from. Writing a historical novel had been a dream for many years, and it was her time now.

She was comfortable financially, but life had been difficult. It was time to seize this opportunity and make the most of it. She'd been half joking last year when she'd told Megan and David she was going to write, but once she'd mentioned it, the idea had stayed and grown.

The sceptical looks she'd received should have been enough to dissuade her, but the more she thought about it. the more she decided to take time off from a real job, the more the idea had appealed.

Even if she was never published, it would be a satisfying achievement to write—and complete—a whole book.

The past few years of historical research and formal theses had given her a good grounding in expressing herself, but the research had been dry at times. The temptation of being able to combine her historical knowledge and give her imagination free rein was one that had been in her mind for a couple of years. Besides mentioning it to David and Megan, she'd only shared her dream with one other person. Phillip's laughter should have been enough for her to know they weren't right together.

Enough.

Beth focused on the present. 'Have you always lived in Somerset,' she asked the taxi driver as he glanced over when she sighed.

'Aye,' he nodded. 'And my father, and grandfather and great-grandfather before me.'

'My great-aunt lived here. I'm going to stay in her cottage.'

'I think I know the one you're talking about. There's two cottages side-by side up that way: Violet Cottage and Rose Cottage, I think they're called.'

'That's them.'

'You're a ways from the village. Is anyone expecting you?'

'No.'

'What about milk and bread. How about I stop in the village so you can get some things? It'll be too dark to walk in tonight. And no extra charge, luv. You're my last fare today. And I live not far from Pilton, meself.'

'Thank you.' Beth's certainty that she had made the right decision grew. 'That would be very kind of you.'

Chapter 4

'Megan, for God's sake, stop worrying.' David's voice was full of rare exasperation, and Silas Rogers shot him a curious glance before he crossed to the window. He and David had been close for a long time, but Silas had seen a change in him since he and Megan had been together. He frowned as he waited to see what was upsetting David; the weather outside was depressing. The snow was falling fast now and the artificial lake at the front of the castle had frozen solid.

Great weather for a wedding.

'I hope your Aussie guests know how ball-breaking cold it is in this castle.' Silas turned to Megan as she crossed the huge ballroom and joined him at the window.

'I know, but I warned them all. The problem is they're coming from the middle of a heat wave back home so it's going to be an extra shock to them.' She smiled and waved a hand towards the Christmas card scene outside. 'But it's so beautiful, isn't it?'

'I'm sorry I snapped.' David came and stood beside her and dropped a kiss on her lips as she looked up at him. 'It is beautiful, darling.' He turned to Silas. 'I hope you weren't too disappointed when we changed the venue from the island to here, Slim.'

'Not disappointed, but curious. A tropical beach or a thirteenth century castle in the Highlands. No choice, hey, bro?'

'You taking the piss out of me, Slim?' David thumped him on his upper arm.

'Me? No way. This is a spectacular venue for a rock star wedding. Snow, bitter cold, and a draughty castle. Inspiring. I even feel a song coming on.' Silas put on chattering teeth and started to sing. 'C-c-c-cold love . . . k-k-k-keeps me. . .'

David rolled his eyes. 'You don't have to stay.'

'You know he does.' Megan put her hand on David's arm. 'Have you asked Slim yet?'

'Asked me what?' Silas narrowed his eyes, before he grinned. 'I knew it. You want me to be best man!'

'Of course I do. That goes without saying. I thought I'd already asked you, anyway.'

'You did. I've got my monkey suit up in the room.'

'David? Go on, ask please.' Megan's voice was soft. 'Until I know Beth is going to be looked after, I can't concentrate on the wedding preparations.'

'What do you have to do?' David reached out and pulled Megan in for a close hug. 'I thought we'd hired enough help. There shouldn't be anything left to worry about, sweetheart.'

'It's all wonderful.' Megan's expression relaxed for a moment. 'Thank you. I'm still not used to this.' She reached up and put her hand on David's cheek. The look in Megan's eyes as she held her future husband's gaze, set a strange feeling loose in Silas's gut.

'But until I know Beth's safe—and will stay safe— I can't relax. The thought of her down there in the cottage is keeping me awake at night. I know she's only there three nights or so before we get her up here, but still—'

'It's okay. I've got a plan,' David replied. 'She'll be fine until she goes back home to Australia.'

Silas had known David for a long time, and he knew the look that crossed his friend's face was one that he should be worried about. He put his hands up and backed away. 'Hey, man. I know that look, and I know it means you're going to ask me to do something I don't want to do.'

David shook his head. 'It's nothing like you think. It just means you have to stay here a bit longer after the wedding.'

'Here? Here as in the castle?' He nodded and looked around at the huge ball room. 'I could cope with that. I can play guitar as loud as I want and there'll be no one to complain. After the wedding guests have gone anyway.'

'No, not here in the castle.'

'So where's here?' Silas frowned as David stared at him. 'I've got a feeling I'm not going to like this.'

'Not here, like as in where. But here as in "now".'

Silas scowled. 'So stay for how long? And where?''

'Back down at Glastonbury. At the cottage. Beth'll only be here a couple of weeks, won't she, Megan?'

The tell-tale flush on her cheeks told Silas he wasn't going to like Megan's answer either.

'Um . . .' Megan said.

'Um?' David replied.

'Um, I think she's staying for a few months at least.'

'Shit!' David slammed his fist into his hand. 'She can't. I was going to ask Slim to babysit Beth for a couple of weeks, and make sure she doesn't go wandering. I've had a high fence built across the back of the cottages. You have to go the long way around now to get to the stones.' He shook his head. 'But Slim, I can't expect you to stay months.'

Slim shrugged. 'I've got nothing to go home for. I can write songs and rehearse for our gigs anywhere. As long as the neighbour doesn't mind the music.' He looked at Davy. 'And I'm thinking about following your lead?'

'My lead?'

'Staying here for good. There's not a lot back there for me now. You're here. Bear's gone.'

'We'd like that, Slim.' David lifted his head and held Silas's gaze. 'And thank you. It would be a great help. I think you'll need to keep a close eye from something Beth said when we were in Sydney

'Oh?' Silas straightened his shoulders. 'What was that?'

'She read some of Alice's journals, when she was here a while back. Ten years ago actually, just after Alice passed on. And she reckons she is going to write a novel based on her great aunt's experiences.'

'Oh.' Silas's head flew up. 'Not good.'

David nodded. 'Not good at all. I want you to stick to her like a leech. If you hear that front door open I want you out like a shot. You can stay in my cottage next door.'

'Okay. I'll help out as best I can.' Even though there was no one apart from David and Megan in the room, Silas lowered his voice. 'How much does she know?'

David and Megan shrugged together. 'That's the problem. We don't know. It's going to be up to you to find out.'

Silas leaned back against the window and the cold of the glass came through his hoodie. 'Without giving anything away? That's going to be interesting.'

Chapter

The sleet began not long after the taxi dropped her off, and Beth was doubly grateful to the taxi driver—who she now knew as Reg—for being so thoughtful. It turned out he knew Great Aunt Alice, and there was some family relationship about three times removed. He'd stopped in Pilton, the closest village, and waited outside the small shop while she picked up some basic provisions that would last until she headed north to the wedding in a couple of days. The shopkeeper had been very friendly.

'Hello, and welcome! I'm Jules.' The elderly woman held out a hand and Beth shook it. 'You're staying in Alice's cottage then?'

Beth nodded. 'I am for a few days and then I'm heading up to Scotland for a wedding.' Megan had told her about Jules the shopkeeper who would warn her about all manner of things.

Jules nodded. 'Megan and Davy's wedding. Some of the villagers have been invited too.' She pulled a sad face. 'I would have loved to have gone, but I can't leave the store.' She nodded out the back. 'My better half's not interested in the shop at all. Lazy oaf, he is. So what can I get for you, love?' She nodded and the strange purple hat on her head bobbed. 'Tea? Milk, bread, butter? I've got a little essentials pack made up for you here. I heard you were coming today.'

'That's very kind of you,' Beth said with a frown. As far as she knew, no one in the village could have known when she was arriving.

Jules chatted nonstop as she put the groceries into a large brown paper bag.

'So you know there's no Wi-Fi, no landline, and cell service down your lane is spotty.' The grooves on either side of the woman's mouth deepened as she frowned. 'The magnetics have been on the rise more than usual this winter. It's the cold weather coming on. And that cottage is way too close to—' She broke off and waved a hand. 'But you'll find all that out yourself.'

Beth nodded and smiled as she paid for the goods and took the bag.

'Oh and if Alice makes an appearance'—the woman tapped the side of her nose and the crazy hat bobbed again—'and I have no doubt she will, don't be scared. She's harmless. So say hello from me. It were her that told me you were coming today.'

'Thank you.' Beth hurried from the store. She couldn't imagine Megan and David inviting the local storekeeper to the wedding.

The drive to the cottage only took a few minutes, but it would have been too far to carry groceries.

'You survived Jules okay?' Reg lifted his nose to the fast darkening sky as she went around to the back of the taxi to unload her bags.'

'Yes, she seems a bit of a character,' Beth said slowly.

'Always has been,' Reg said. 'But she's got worse since Ted died. He used to help her out in the shop.'

'Ted?'

'Her husband. Got pneumonia and shuffled off last winter. So you make sure you keep yourself warm. I hope you've got plenty of firewood in there. It's going to turn cold. I can smell snow.'

Despite her thoughts about the crazy shopkeeper, Beth couldn't help clapping her hands. 'Oh, how wonderful. My first white Christmas.'

'You got others coming to stay with you?' He looked at her curiously.

Beth didn't want the fact that she was here alone to get around. 'Yes, there will be someone else arriving.' Her words were confident and friendly, even though she had no idea who was going to arrive to whisk her to the north in a couple of days. Spending Christmas alone didn't bother her in the slightest. It would be easier and much more pleasant than dividing her time between Mum and a restaurant, and Dad and his new wife.

She waved Reg off and unlocked the door with the key that Mum had given her. Her nerves jigged with anticipation as she pushed open the door and turned the light switch on. Beth let out a sigh of pleasure as the door closed behind her and she leaned against it looking around, absorbing the familiar smell and sight of the cottage she'd visited such a long time ago.

The room was exactly the same as it had been ten years ago. A musty smell pervaded the small living room. She left her bags inside the door and walked over and looked in the firebox. A small pile of dry logs and split kindling half-filled the metal box. And just as Beth remembered, a box of extra-long matches sat on the mantlepiece. Soon she had a small fire crackling in the grate, and the sharp aroma of pine logs soon dispelled the mustiness of the cottage that had been closed up since Megan had visited a few months back. In the end Mum hadn't let the cottage, but had made it available to friends and family who travelled to the UK. Beth had been pleased; it had been her father who had wanted to sell it. Whenever Beth had tried to talk to Mum about the cottage and the curious appeal it held for her, she'd always change the subject.

The long journey had taken its toll and after nodding over a cup of tea, Beth put one of her bags in one of the small bedrooms at the top of the stairs before she had a quick wash in the tiny bathroom. A marble washstand took up most to the wall and a free standing bath sat beneath the window. A pretty jug covered in pink flowers with an ornate curly handle sat in a dish on the washstand.

She was too tired to make the bed up with sheets; with a wide yawn she pulled out her warm pyjamas and thick dressing gown, and when dressed, crawled under the down comforter on the soft bed.

As her eyelids closed, the feeling of excited anticipation stayed firmly in her chest.

It only seemed a short while later, but fingers of pale, watery sunlight were trying to make a mark on the bedroom wall when Beth opened her eyes. Happiness flooded through her as she remembered where she was. She turned over onto her back and stretched, and couldn't keep the smile from her face as she stared around the room. There were no sounds to be heard; no birds singing, no voices and no traffic going down the small lane past the cottage. When she'd arrived last night the other cottage had been in darkness.

Her satisfaction grew as she swung her legs over the bed. Her feet touched the floorboards and she gasped. Reaching for the socks she'd discarded last night, Beth pulled them over cold toes, and then she padded across to the window. She drew a breath in as the idyllic scene filled her vision.

'Oh, how gorgeous,' she whispered to herself. The fields were white and the tree branches bowed with the weight of the snow that had fallen while she'd slept. Just as well Reg had insisted on taking her to the shop; she could bunker down in the cottage without needing to go out. Two whole days of uninterrupted reading beckoned as soon as she'd unpacked and organised the cottage.

Guilt trickled though her; it would be good if she could stay here uninterrupted. Maybe the roads would be impassable from the snowfall. And she could stay here and read instead of going to Scotland.

'No.' Beth shook herself and pushed away those thoughts. Megan was her best friend, and they'd been through a lot together.

Beth had supported Megan when all those awful accusations had been made against her last year, and when she had lost her parents in that horrific road accident.

Megan had reciprocated when Beth had needed support, and her sensible—and often humorous, if not sarcastic—suggestions had made the situation with Phillip much easier to cope with. Megan hadn't liked Phillip from the day that Beth had introduced him to her, and she'd picked him for the conniving lowlife that he was.

Forget it. Move on.

But it was hard. Phillip's actions, plus the deterioration of her parents' marriage had destroyed her faith in people and left Beth unwilling to trust.

Megan had picked up the pieces, and a night of ice-cream and champagne when Beth had discovered Phillip's perfidy had made their friendship even stronger. So of course she wanted to go to the wedding and be there when Megan married the love of her life, David Morgan.

It didn't take her long to shower and dress, and then unpack her two suitcases. She sang softly beneath her breath as she put her clothes away. The last job she had to do upstairs was hang the dress she'd bought for the wedding.

Glamorous *and* warm—the dress was as Megan had instructed. Beth stepped back and nodded as she smoothed the emerald-green velvet dress. The velvet was soft beneath her fingers as she slipped it onto the padded hangar she found in the wardrobe.

The long dress had been a fortuitous find at Shabby-Chic, a retro shop at Paddington in Sydney—much to her mother's dismay—and it was certainly warm.

'You can't wear a second-hand dress to a wedding!'

'Oh yes I can. This is just perfect.' Beth had looked down at the long sleeves that tapered to a point at the edge of her wrist. A sweetheart neckline above a fitted bodice added to its elegance. It was almost medieval and she couldn't wait to wear it.

The dress had fitted her like a glove, and needed no alterations Ginny Silver, the store owner had called her a couple of weeks later.

'Beth, I've found a pair of emerald green shoes to match the dress.'

With a final glance at the dress hanging from the curtain rod in the small bedroom, Beth shook her head in disbelief. She was in England, and heading off to a celebrity wedding at Rothmore Castle in Scotland.

Her smile got wider as she headed downstairs to the cellar where there was a trunkful of journals waiting to be read.

Chapter 6

It was a long time before I travelled again.

Seven years.

Seven endless years of heart-numbing grief, and wondering if I should have stayed.

The grief of leaving Branton behind had been unbearable, and when I came home to the cottage, I immersed myself in volunteer work. I Joined the Land Army; during the war, there was always plenty to do, and I trained at Cannington Farm as a land girl. It was easier for me than many of the young women who came down from London, but it was safer than being in the city with the daily bombings.

It was bad enough in the country, and even Somerset was bombed. The farm I was allocated to was three miles out of Yeovil and beneath the flight path of the German bombers coming from the west of France. Air raid sirens became a part of our lives, but strangely my grief made me immune to the reactions of those around me. At that time of my life, death held no fear for me. It wasn't until the war was over that I managed to pull myself out of the numb state where I spent much of those years. Wearying years where a sense of desperate urgency held the population in its relentless grip, then stolid endurance through the Blitz, and the ever-growing fear of invasion. But then the tide turned as hope came from a North African victory, and we began to believe the tide had turned at last.

In a way, volunteering eased my guilt at having gone away when the war began. I wasn't being a coward; none of us expected the war to last for so long. No one had imagined the bombing, and the damage to our countryside. The displaced children, and the lack of me to work the farms.

Toiling alongside other young women in the field, helped me forget and some days I managed to go for hours without thinking of what I had left behind.

Perhaps I should have stayed.

If I had stayed, our child may have survived.

Time is fleeting. Seize each opportunity. Make the most of every minute.

##

Beth drew her breath in on a gasp, and then jumped as her phone trilled its familiar ring tone. She had been alone for over twenty-four hours, and hadn't spoken to a soul. She'd sent a quick email to her parents and to Megan letting them know she'd arrived safely. Contrary to Jules' assumption, the Wi-Fi and now it appeared, the phone service to, had been fine.

She picked up the phone and pressed it to her hear, her eyes still skimming over the spidery hand writing in front of her.

'Merry Christmas, Beth.'

'Hello, Mum. And the same to you, although it's still Christmas Eve here.'

'You've settled in then? How long until you leave for Scotland?'

'I'm just waiting to hear a definite time from Megan.'

'Have you decided where you'll go after the wedding? There's so much to see there.' Her mother's voice held a tinge of worry, and Beth bit back a sigh as she persisted. 'Make sure you spend some time in Edinburgh. There's so much history there. You'll love it. I did, but your father wasn't impressed. All he could talk about was the dirty buildings!'

Beth narrowed her eyes. 'When were you in Edinburgh? I didn't think you'd ever been to Scotland.'

Her mother took a while to answer, but finally she did and her words were soft. 'Your father and I went over to visit Alice not long after we were married. Before you were born.'

'You never mentioned that. I thought our trip after she died was your first visit.'

'I don't know why you thought that.'

Because that's what you told me, Beth thought to herself, but didn't articulate it.

'Alice had some . . . er . . . problems, and we went over to help her sort them out.

'Mum, how old was Great-Aunt Alice when she died? Or do you know what year she was born? Do you know anything about her life? Was she married?'

'Why do you want to know all that? I know enough to tell you that things need to be left alone. You've been reading those bloody diaries, haven't you?' Suddenly, a viciousness entered her mother's tone. 'Leave. Them. Alone. Do you hear me, Beth?'

'Why?' Beth sat up straighter on the sofa, and grabbed for the cushions that rolled over her lap.

'Because it does no good raking over the past. She was a sad and lonely woman.' Now she changed to a persuasive soft voice. 'I would be so much happier if you left the cottage, Beth darling. It's not a good place to be. I wasn't going to tell you that Alice suffered significant mental health issues, and we had to go over that first time, because she was so very unwell.'

'What sort of unwell?' Beth thought of the words she'd read; the Second World War had been over for five years before her mother had been born, so it wasn't what she'd been reading about today.

'She suffered from hallucinations, delusions, some sort of psychotic disorder. When we went over there before you were born, we had her admitted.'

'Mum! You never told me that.'

'There was never any need for you to know. I'm just sorry we took you over there ten years ago and you developed this stupid fascination with the place.'

'It's not stupid.'

'Well, then you tell me what it is? It's unhealthy. What's the point of a woman your age traipsing about the English countryside, chasing a dream? You should be married to Phillip, and giving me grandchildren. I'm over it, Beth, You need to get back here, and make up with Phillip and come to your senses.'

For a few seconds Beth considered disconnecting the call. She swallowed and counted to ten, gripping the cushion tightly with her other hand.

'I'm going to forget that you said that, Mum.' Her voice was level as she fought for calm. 'And I'm going to wish you a Merry Christmas and then I'm going to bed. I'll call you when I get to Scotland. Go and have another Christmas wine.' Even though it was probably before lunch in

Australia, she could hear the occasional slur in her mother's words. She'd started the champagne early today.

'Bethie—'

'Goodbye, Mum.' She hit the end button and then switched her phone off. She knew her mother too well. She'd keep ringing and ringing until she got her own way.

But this time Beth wasn't going to give in for the sake of peace or to make her mother happy. The words she'd dropped about Phillip had cut deep. Beth was healing and wasn't about to revisit it. Her self-esteem had been shot, and it had taken many months and a good talking to from Megan to make her realise that she wasn't at fault.

It was easier to immerse herself in the past, than focus on the cruel words that her mother had uttered.

Was it the past? Or was it fiction? The scribblings of a—perhaps—disturbed mind?'

Beth picked up the journal, and flicked through the pages, looking for a date or a name.

Maybe they didn't even belong to Alice? Maybe it was someone else who had written the words. Made-up stories? Stories maybe based on some fact, or stories that were totally fiction. A glimmer of an idea began to take root. With her historical connections, it wouldn't be too hard to research some of the things she'd read today. There were place names—Cannington Farm—that she could research, and see if what was written was true. There would be war records and she could check if it is was Alice McLaren who had worked as a land girl.

She wanted to know.

Beth stood and walked into the kitchen. It was late, and the cottage was getting colder. A wind had picked up, and the creaks and groans of the old cottage, and the tree branches rubbing against the roof unsettled her for the first time. She crossed to the window. It was pitch dark outside, not even any starlight to break the dark sky above. As she stood in the dark of the kitchen staring outside, a faint light caught her attention. There was a narrow gap in the high fence at the bottom of the garden, and a light had crossed the field past that gap.

Beth frowned and stepped back from the window. She walked back into the living room and turned her phone on to check the time. It was a minute before midnight; she hadn't realised how late it was as she'd sat there reading after the soup and toast dinner she'd had earlier.

She hurried up the stairs; it was easier to see above the high fence from the window in the bedroom. There were no roads or lanes out the back, and it was unlikely that anyone would be crossing the field in the middle of the night. There was a path across the fields to the village, but it only led to the two cottages and the one next door had been empty since she'd arrived. Beth knew it belonged to David—that's how he and Megan had met—and as far as she was aware there was no one staying there.

Leaving the lights off, she pulled the curtains open and stood there looking in the direction of where the light had flashed briefly. It was dark, and there was no sign of anyone walking with a torch. The snow was falling in soft white flakes and again she wondered if she'd get to Scotland.

As Beth lifted her hand to pull the curtain closed, a blue flash lit up the night sky. It shot up in an arc from the middle of the field at the back of the cottage, so bright, that for a moment, she'd seen Glastonbury Tor to the west.

Or she thought she had. She blinked and rubbed a hand over her eyes. It was pitch dark again outside and there was no movement and no bright blue light.

It took a lot longer to get to sleep tonight than it had yesterday.

Chapter 7

'Are you sure you don't mind driving all the way down to Somerset, Slim?' David Morgan lifted his guitar strap over his head and settled the guitar across his hips. 'I could hire a firm out of London.'

'No, not at all. It's not that far down there, and if I take my Land Rover, it'll be safer in the snow than your Bentley. Besides, wherever I go in this place I seem to be getting in the way of someone putting up some decoration or moving a table, or carrying some bit of furniture from room to room.'

David grinned as he picked at the strings. 'Yeah, I think even Megan's over it. Kathy's taken over as the wedding planner, and she's in her element. We're grinning and bearing it.'

'It'll be a good event. I like Kathy too.'

'Yeah, they're pretty close sisters. It's going to be strange to be part of a family. A sister-in-law and a brother-in-law and a readymade nephew.'

Silas shook his head. 'So a married man, hey? That'll be the end of the rock star antics on stage at Glastonbury next year.'

'I've decided I wasn't going to go anyway.' David played a chord and it hung in the air as he held Slim's gaze. 'I'm not going back again. I'm not prepared to risk it. And that's not for general consumption yet. ' He cleared his throat. 'Megan's having a baby.'

'Oh, wow, man.' Silas was embarrassed when moisture filled his eyes and he blinked. He and David—and Bear who was now gone—had been together for a long time. 'Well, wow again. You're gonna be a dad.' He looked at David curiously. 'You really mean that? About the festival? You're not going there again?'

'No. If I'm wanted, I'll play at the contemporary festivals, but I'm not prepared to take the risk of getting lost. Not now. It didn't matter before.' His close friend, and leader of the band they'd played in together, stared at him. 'Do you mind?'

Slim turned away and shook his head. 'Not really, Davy. There's nothing to keep me in either place. Alice is gone, Bear's gone. My olds have gone. You're about it for me. And Megan now.' He knew he sounded pathetic, but what he'd said was true. The band had been his life, and as long as he could play guitar he could happily live anywhere. 'You want me to do that babysitting job after the wedding at the cottage, so I'll hang around for a while at least.'

Silas was surprised when David brushed the back of his hand across his eyes. 'Well, make sure you say goodbye, if you do decide to leave,' he said gruffly. 'I've got used to you being around. And thanks, Slim, for the babysitting. Maybe she won't figure it out, but if she does I want you to stop her.'

'We can hope.' He nodded. 'And you have my word.'

##

It was good to get away from Scotland although Silas was surprised; it was just as cold down south as it had been at Rothmore Castle. Bloody great fires in all the cavernous rooms had done nothing to heat the cold stone. It had been a white Christmas all right. A bloody cold, white Christmas, but he'd enjoyed spending the time with David and Megan, and her sister, Kathy, and her husband, Tony. Even their little bub had been cute.

He shook his head as he changed back a gear. So Davy was going to be a dad. Since Megan had met Davy at Glastonbury last June, change had been in the wind. He'd sensed it in David's music, and he could tell by seeing the way David looked at his woman. Since Bear had died suddenly in the spring, nothing had been the same. The band wasn't the same. His life wasn't the same.

Silas knew he had some big decisions to make; it didn't matter to him where he was, as long as he could make music. Maybe he could stay here and find another lead guitarist and singer, and a drummer. Maybe he could start another band. His mood closed in around him and he reached down to turn the heat up in the Land Rover. He was thirty-five, too old to start out again, and he wondered if he still had the energy.

As he left the motorway and skirted around Birmingham towards Somerset, Slim tried to figure out where his priorities were. He knew that David and Megan would leave the UK; that was a given, and no matter what David had said he doubted whether David would come back to perform at all.

Maybe I could just retire from performing, and simply write. Hell, he didn't need the money. They'd sold enough albums to keep them in the style to which they'd become quickly accustomed, for life.

If he admitted the truth to himself, Silas knew he was lost, and he needed to do some serious thinking before he went anywhere.

Chapter 8

Beth had been unsettled since last night. She'd set aside the journals, and spent some time outside shovelling snow off the path—a totally new experience for her, but one she'd found satisfying and invigorating. As she'd stood at the window looking out this morning while she waited for the kettle to boil on the Aga, her mobile had trilled and she picked it up reluctantly, expecting it to be Mum again, with more nagging.

'Beth, it's Meg.' Her friend didn't even give her time for a greeting. 'I got your email. I'm pleased you found the place okay and everything was okay there. A bit musty, I'd say. I just rang to tell you—'

Beth laughed. 'Slow down, Megs. Are you even going to give me a chance to say hello?

Megan giggled at the other end of the phone. 'Okay, let's start again. Hello Beth, it's Megan.'

'Hi Megan.' Beth chuckled. 'I haven't heard you sound so happy for a long time. Wedding all organised?'

'God, yes. Kathy's organised everyone to within an inch of their lives. She's even organised for the waitresses to wear the Rothmore tartan. I don't know what the rules are about wearing tartan, but I didn't have time to find out. Maybe you could look it up and tell me. Anyway I just rang to tell you that Slim—Silas—will be there to pick you up this afternoon. He left pretty early this morning.'

'Silas from the band?' Beth's voice choked on a squeak.

'Yep, Slim, Davy's best man.'

'Eek, Megs, what am I going to talk to him about? How many hours is the drive?'

'It's about seven hours if you get a good run. Slim knows the shortcuts. And talk to him about what you'd talk to anyone else about.'

'He's a rock star!'

'Don't be silly. Slim is just Slim. He's not up himself, so don't worry about that. He's a great guy, a bit eccentric, but a good person. He left early so he should be there about mid-afternoon. He's going to stay in Davy's cottage and then you can both leave first thing tomorrow. '

'Okay. Are you getting excited?'

'Oh, Beth, I can't put into words how wonderful it is. How happy I am. It's–' Her voice trembled with emotion.

Beth knew Megan well enough; there was something else there. 'But you wish your mum and dad were going to be there?'

There was no response for a few seconds.

'You're a good friend, sweets. Yes, I have been a bit upset about it. Kathy gave me a talking to when I had a good cry the other morning. My emotions have been all over the place.'

'Don't worry, 'sensible Beth' will be there soon to sort you out.'

'I can't wait to see you.' Megan's voice was full of excitement. 'I've got so much to tell you. But enough of that, tell me what you've been up to. You haven't been too lonely or bored in the cottage? What's the weather like? Have you been to the village?'

'Um, let me see.' Beth chuckled. 'No and no. Cold. And yes.'

'You've been to the village?'

'Only on the way in the other night. The cab driver was a local and he took pity on me. Just as well, because the snow's been too heavy to go walking.'

'So you've stayed in the cottage the whole time. And you're not lonely?'

'No. I'm loving it. I've decided to stay for a long visit.'

'How long for? Do you think that's really a good idea?'

Beth was taken aback at the hesitation in Megan's voice. 'God, Megan, don't you start. I've had Mum on my case. At the airport, and on the phone last night.'

'Beth, everyone wants what's best for you.'

'Okay, then.' Beth kept her tone upbeat, even though she couldn't understand why Megan had a problem with her staying longer. 'We'll talk about it when I get there. So I guess I'll see you tomorrow?'

'You will. Oh, Beth, wait until you see this place. Can you believe it? I'm still pinching myself. Megan Miller from Sydney is getting married to a rock star in a Scottish castle!'

'I can. Now tell me who's going to be there and whether I'm going to be star struck or not.'

They chatted and laughed for another fifteen minutes, and Beth's worry had lessened a fraction by the time they ended the call.

Megan's reaction to her extending her stay had concerned Beth, and the idea of travelling up to Scotland with one of the members of David Morgan's famous band had thrown her for a minute or two.

She took a deep breath, and told herself that worrying never solved anything. She'd deal with both situations when she had to.

The best way to lose herself and stop worrying was to get into the journals again. She'd be gone for a few days, and had even considered taking one with her to read at night. Beth glanced at her watch. She imagined that this Silas would call in and let her know he had arrived, even if they weren't heading north until the morning. She glanced at her watch. If she packed now, she could spend the time tonight reading and getting her thoughts in order.

Both her mother's and Megan's attitudes had bothered her. She had to have a plan; not only to appease their concerns—concerns that she couldn't understand—but she needed to work out what she was going to do with the journals.

As well as writing a novel, she could do some more research, and use them for a historical study? If she read and assessed the various entries in the journals, and decided that they were legitimate primary accounts of historical periods, she could transcribe them and give them to a museum, or even publish her own nonfiction book.

If it ensued that they were merely stories from the imagination of Great Aunt Alice, she could stick with her original idea of writing a novel. Until she had been through all of the books in the trunk in the cellar, she couldn't make her decision.

But whatever her decision was, she was staying here and not going back to Australia for a very long time. The thought of giving in and going back to the university, and working in the same faculty as Phillip, made her feel ill.

Beth hurried upstairs and quickly packed one of her suitcases, making sure she packed the warmest clothes she'd brought. She left it open and put it on the floor beneath where the velvet dress hung on the curtain rail, before she headed down to the cellar.

Chapter 9

Joy filled me as the prospect of seeing Branton again thrummed in my heart. I had travelled widely before I went back to Glastonbury. When I first arrived, I was still unsure so I took the time to travel throughout England. Only another week and I would be with him again.

Arrived from where? Beth wondered.

London was a very interesting experience, but now it was time to make my way to Glastonbury.

The risk of travelling widely had been worth it; as well as seeing the way the country was, I had time to think more on returning to Branton.

I was on my way. The coach departed from Blackheath and I was making my way to the inn. Much soul searching, and six months of planning and putting my affairs in order, and now I was ready to see Branton and commit to him. I had no fear that he would not be waiting for me. He had promised he would wait if I changed my mind, had given me his heart and I knew he would be happy that I had returned to him.

I longed to see the roses and the honeysuckle that climbed his manor house, almost as much as I longed to see Branton. I thought that I would have many years to see that.

This time I would stay, and make my life with him. It had taken many, many hours of soul searching to come to that decision, but the love I held for him in my heart was too strong to ignore. I knew it was a lifetime but—

Suddenly a huge whoosh and a deafening noise filled the air around me.

I ran. I pushed through the hedgerow into the field beside the road in case there was another explosion.

I backed away as the hoarse cries of men in pain surrounded me. Dozens of men lay on the ground in front of me. I tried to lift my feet but the mud that had been churned by many feet held my leather shoes like a steel vice.

I raised a shaking hand to my lips, and stifled a cry. One moment I had been walking alone towards the inn, and thinking of the delightful reunion two day ahead, and then I had been thrown off my feet by an explosion and a force so strong my chest still ached.

The scene before me was carnage such as I had never witnessed before. It was like the photos that I had seen of the battlefields in the First World War, in the trenches of France where my father had perished.

As I stood there, a young man, no older than my sister's son, rolled over onto his back and held his hands out to me, beseeching me to help him. His face was a rictus of pain and blood dripped into his eyes.

I closed my eyes wondering if it was all a dream. Maybe I hadn't come here after all, but the heartrending cries could not have come from my imagination or dreams. I sank to the ground, not caring about the cold mud on my skirts, and I held out my hands to comfort the dying young man.

IT was a full week before I made my way to Glastonbury and the manor house, but it was empty. The door was locked and there was no smoke from the chimneys, the house was in disrepair and it looked as though it hadn't been lived in for many weeks.

I knocked but there was no one there. The stables were empty, and there was no life anywhere.

No chickens pecking the grass around the stables, and the fields were empty of sheep.

Branton was gone.

I choked back my despair as I retraced my steps towards home.

Chapter 10

Beth's eyes were wet with tears and her hand shook as she closed the journal.

Where had Alice been?

Or what had she been creating from her imagination? The fear and the despair had been so real, it sat heavily in Beth's chest as Alice had described.

Beth closed her eyes and put her hand to her heart. The last words had been smudged, and she knew instinctively that Alice had shed tears on the page as she had written them.

'Hello?'

She lifted her head as someone banged on the kitchen door. Quickly rubbing at her eyes with a tissue she had shoved deep in her pocket, she stood and placed the journal carefully on the sofa. She glanced at the clock on the kitchen wall, even as she was surprised to see the afternoon light fading quickly as she headed for the back of the cottage.

She opened the door slowly and peered around, wondering who would be knocking. She stepped back and looked up as her gaze first encountered a throat encased in a tartan scarf.

Her eyes travelled slowly up past the scarf, up past a firm chin, ruddy cheeks to finally settle on a pair of deep blue eyes, holding concern.

'Hello, you *are* Beth, I hope?' The voice was deep with a strong accent that clipped his words.

She nodded as she stared back at him. 'Um, yes, I'm Beth McLaren. You must be Silas.'

His eyes crinkled in a smile as he nodded back. 'That I am. Silas Rogers, your chauffeur. I knocked at the front; I thought you must have been out.'

'Oh, I'm sorry. I lost track of the time, I was reading.' She pulled the door open wider. 'Please come in. That wind is icy.'

'No. I won't. That is if you don't mind. It's been a long drive, and I'm going to hit the sack early. I just wanted to let you know we'll leave as soon as it's light tomorrow.'

'I'll be ready. I'm all packed. Thanks so much for coming down to get me. I told Megan I could have got the train north.' Beth couldn't take her eyes off his face as the words babbled from her lips. A lock of jet-black hair fell over a high forehead, and he reached up to push it back. His skin was fair, but it was the deep blue eyes fringed with long dark lashes that held her attention.

'No. It was no trouble at all.' He dropped his voice and tapped his cheek with a long finger. His fingernails were clipped square, and Beth couldn't help thinking what elegant hands he had. The silence was awkward as they both stood there, not speaking and just looking at each other, until finally he stepped back. 'Well, I'll be seeing you in the morning then. If you are ready by seven that would be good.'

Beth nodded, feeling like a gauche adolescent. 'Thank you, again. I'll see you tomorrow.'

She closed the door quietly after he disappeared around the side of the cottage. Leaning against the back of the door, she took a deep breath.

Silas Rogers might be a member of Davy Morgan's famous band, but she'd never seen a photo of him. His good looks and his cultured demeanour had come as a surprise; she hadn't really given him much thought, but he wasn't what she would have expected.

And now she had to sit in a car with him, and make conversation for the whole day. She'd been barely able to stop babbling in the few minutes he'd been here, until that uncomfortable silence. He'd probably been wondering what he'd volunteered for.

Beth closed her eyes as she looked down at the pink dressing gown she was wearing and the fluffy socks. Her nose would be red and her eyes puffy after the tears she'd shed when Aunt Alice's words had got to her.

##

'You could have warned me, mate.' Silas leaned back against the back door enjoying the quiet of the evening. The wind had dropped, the sky had cleared and moonlight lit the snow in the back garden. He patted his pocket looking for a cigarette and then remembered he'd given it up.

'What about?' David asked. The phone connection was scratchy and Silas had to concentrate to hear David's reply.

'What a stunner Beth is. Drop dead gorgeous with all that red hair and fair skin.'

'Can't say I've ever taken much notice. She's a nice person, and she's been a good friend to Megan.'

'You've been so smitten with Megan, I'm not surprised you haven't noticed. The old Davy Morgan has disappeared, that's for sure.'

David's chuckle came through clearly. 'So you won't mind doing that babysitting job after the wedding when she goes back to the cottage then?'

'If you think it's necessary.'

'It is, mate. 'Megan said she's all fired up reading Alice's diaries. It's only a matter of time before she twigs. It's not safe.'

'I'll have to stick to her like glue, if she goes wandering out the back.' Silas stared at the high fence that Davy had hired a contractor from Taunton to build. 'I don't know that your fence is going to work.'

'Better than nothing. It might stop anyone wandering over that way. I'll never forget when Megan followed me last year.'

'She was lucky she ended up where she did.'

'I know. It's been getting harder each time. And I know Alice had some pretty bad experiences. The problem is I don't know what she's documented. I didn't know she'd written anything down until Megan told me that's why Beth's staying there. Apparently there's a trunk full of books. Alice was a quiet and private person, but that's not to say she didn't document her journeys.'

'I'll see what I can find out on the way up. Maybe there's nothing to worry about.'

'Thanks. Appreciate it. And enjoy the trip.'

Silas slipped the phone into his pocket and tilted his head to the side. A familiar low hum was coming across the field and he glanced at his watch. It was a few seconds before midnight.

He waited, his arms stiff by his side and his hands clenched. No matter how many times he came through, the thought of it still did his head in. Right on cue, a blue flash lit up the night sky and goose bumps ran up his arms.

Noon and midnight.

The humming stopped and all was quiet again until the mooing of a lonely cow broke the silence.

Silas turned for the door and let himself in, more unsettled than he had been for a while.

Stay or go? That's what he had to figure out; he had a lot of thinking ahead of him.

Chapter 11

Beth set the alarm for six a.m. and by the time she'd had a shower and dressed, and made a cup of tea, the first rosy tendrils of dawn were creeping over the horizon. She stood at the kitchen window as the teabag steeped in the boiling water. The snow had stopped falling through the night but the fields were still white.

Picture postcard stuff; she'd never get sick of looking at a view like that. Her bag was at the front door, and the velvet dress was draped over the sofa; she hoped she could lay it out on the back seat of the car. She'd dressed in layers, unsure of how cold it would be travelling through the day. Warm denim jeans tucked into long boots were topped by a pale green angora jumper. Her wool coat was on top of the one small suitcase she'd packed.

Beth glanced across at her handbag as she took her cup of tea into the living room. She hadn't been able to resist; she'd packed one of the smaller journals into her bag. Last night she'd taken a flashlight into the cellar and sat on the cold stone floor until her legs were numb. She'd barely been aware of the cold as she'd picked up each of the journals and flicked through them. Some of the books were filled with the graceful looped writing she'd become familiar with, and some only had six or seven pages of writing.

Excitement had tugged as she'd picked up the last one from the bottom of the trunk. There were dated entries in one of the journals that was almost filled with writing. The first was 1970, and as she flicked through the pages, there was a new section for each year until 1999.

She'd nodded with satisfaction; surely that could only mean one thing. The dates would seem to indicate that this was a chronicle of Alice's life, and that the events written up were fact rather than fiction.

Beth had resisted the temptation to read it last night, knowing she had to be up early, and had a big trip ahead. She'd placed it securely in her handbag to read while she was away.

Maybe even on the journey, if it was difficult to keep a conversation going. She finished her tea, and took the tea cup into the kitchen and rinsed it. It was fully light now, and she glanced at her watch. Seven thirty—Silas had wanted to be on the road by now.

Unable to resist, she went into the living room, and after pulling out the journal settled in the single chair next to the fireplace.

She shivered and pulled a face; not that the fire would keep her warm. Knowing she was leaving the cottage, she'd made sure it had died down overnight. Now the embers were black and cold. Reaching for her coat, she draped it over her legs and settled in to read until he was ready to leave. She flicked through the journal and it opened at a well-thumbed page.

June 1971.

For the first time in many, many years, I feel secure in the knowledge that I have a friend. A true friend. No one will ever replace Branton, but knowing that there is someone who looks out for me, and who would notice if I didn't return, gives me some measure of comfort.

It has taken a long time.

After I lost him, I didn't write my feelings in my journal. It was hard enough to get through each day without reliving the loss. The decision to go back had been a hard one, but to encounter those poor young men, and then to find that Branton too had gone was too hard to write about.

Foolishly I thought that if I didn't put pen to paper, it perhaps wouldn't seem as real.

David is a good neighbour, and I value his friendship, as I believe he does mine. He is a kind man, and has offered to help at times when he could see I was low. The offer of a simple cup of tea, or a random rose picked from the bush in my front garden made me smile when I was sad.

His music gives me much joy, as do his two friends. The short one makes me laugh. I will not call him by that silly name here.

Beth frowned and looked at the date again, before shaking her head. Megan's David must share a family Christian name. And his relation must have been a musician too. Megan hadn't told her much about her David; she didn't know anything about his family.

I must ask her about him and find out about the past family member who had been kind to Alice, Beth thought as she turned her attention back to the page. 1971 was almost fifty years ago. Poor Alice sounded as though she had had a lonely life.

David travels as I do, and I met his two friends the first time they had been here. They weren't terribly impressed with what they saw here now. I have visited them in return, and I must say it is easy to see why they thought that. If I had the choice I would stay there, but as I get older my family would worry if I was out of touch again.

Beth read for another half hour, before she closed the book and put it into her bag; her lift still hadn't eventuated. She stood and walked to the front door and opened it; there was no sign of life from next door. A dark-coloured Land Rover was parked in the lane outside the front gate, and the early sunlight hadn't melted the snow on the roof and windscreen.

She glanced at her watch and bit her lip. Silas had said they would leave earlier than this, but he was the driver and she wondered if she should go and knock on the door.

Undecided for a few moments Beth waited before she tentatively walked down the path. She pushed open the gate and walked towards the other cottage.

The door was closed, the curtains were drawn and all was quiet. Raising her hand, she lifted the brass door knocker and tapped loudly three times.

She stood back and waited.

There was still no sound from inside and the door stayed firmly shut. A niggle of irritation began to form in her chest. If there was one thing she hated it was being late. And another was people who were unreliable. Okay, he might be an eccentric rock star, but he could be punctual. She would have preferred to make her own way to the wedding but Megan had insisted. At this rate it would be well after dark before they reached Scotland. Looking around, she considered her options. There weren't really any apart from raising Silas. She lifted the brass knocker and brought it down hard, and let it knock half a dozen times.

Eventually there was noise from inside and the sound of footsteps reached her. The door opened slowly and Beth's mouth dried. She swallowed and lifted her gaze from the bare chest that filled her vision.

'Um, I'm sorry for waking you, but I thought you wanted to get away at first light?' she said.

Silas lifted one hand and ran it over his eyes, before he squinted and looked outside. 'Shit no, that's fine. *I'm* sorry. Looks like I slept in.' He looked at her blearily as his hand moved up to his hair. As he ran his fingers through the tangles, the muscles in his chest rippled. Beth's gaze dropped again; she couldn't help herself.

Taking a step back she gestured to the sun-filled garden as she tried to ignore the expanse of bare skin in front of her. Broad shoulders, a lean chest tapering down to jeans that were unzipped, that fine V of dark hair . . .

She hastily averted her gaze for the second time. 'Sun's been up for a while,' she said.

'What time is it?' His voice was husky with sleep.

'It's after eight.

'Bloody heck. My phone must have gone flat. I wanted to be well on the road by now.' He looked at her quizzically. 'You're all ready and packed?'

Beth nodded. 'I am.' She resisted the temptation to say she had been for a couple of hours.

'Okay. Give me ten minutes and I'll be ready to go.'

Before Beth could answer, the door closed in her face and she shrugged as she turned away. She had a feeling this was going to be a very long day. So far she wasn't terribly impressed with David's musician friend.

***

Silas muttered to himself as he pulled a T-shirt over his head and zipped up his jeans before hurrying to the bathroom.

'Blasted phone. He'd forgotten what happened to phones and the like near the stones.

He sluiced icy cold water over his face and cupped his hands under the tap and had a quick drink. That would have to do for breakfast. They'd hit the road and he could eat in a couple of hours when they stopped for fuel.

He couldn't believe he'd slept so late. After seeing the light last night, he'd had trouble getting to sleep, and when he'd finally dropped off, his sleep had been broken by crazy dreams. Men lying on a battleground calling for help, and then small children running around the hayfields in the sunshine.

Crazily, he'd woken up and gone down to the kitchen for a glass of water, but when he'd gone back to sleep the dream about the battle had come back; this time it was so intense, he could still smell the blood that had soaked the ground.

He'd stood there looking like a proper twat, asking Beth what time it was. She'd think he was unreliable after he'd stressed how early he wanted to get away.

He grabbed his keys, picked up his leather jacket and looked around; he'd brought nothing else in with him last night. His bag and guitar were still in the car. He'd stow all his gear here when he came back to stay.

If he did. He'd promised David, but he'd see how things panned out over the next few days. Closing the door behind him, Silas headed for the Land Rover. At least the weather had improved.

Beth had already carried her bag out and he opened the back of the car and lifted in.

'All set?'

'I just have to get my dress for the wedding. Is it okay if I lay it flat on the back seat?'

'Sure.' Silas watched as she hurried back to the cottage. He hadn't noticed much about her last night; he'd been too focused on that glorious auburn hair and translucent skin. Now as she walked away, the denim of her tight jeans clung lovingly to long slim legs.

This babysitting gig mightn't be as bad as he'd thought.

Chapter 12

It was well after dark by the time the lights of the Land Rover swooped over a small brick gatehouse at the end of the long road. Beth's eyes widened as she stared at the castle and she felt like pinching herself. Rothmore Castle sat on a small island in the middle of a lake—no, loch—she corrected herself.

The castle was lit up, with spotlights directed on the four towers at each end of the square structure. A series of lights changed colour every few seconds washing the front of the old building in muted pastels.

Beth let out a soft sigh as a photo of David and Megan in a love heart was projected onto the front of the castle. 'Oh wow, look at that.'

'Looks like practice is in full swing for the day after tomorrow,' Silas said in a wry tone. 'It was driving poor David crazy when I left.'

'Looks like it's going to be pretty flash.'

'You haven't seen the half of it,' he commented.

Beth looked at the wide expanse of water between the gatehouse and the castle. 'Ah, so how do we get over there?' She turned to Silas as he cut the engine.

'I'll call David now. He's got a couple of motorboats over there. Someone will come and get us.' His grin was wide as the interior light came on in the car. 'In the old days, the laird used to row across.' He pulled out his phone and the call picked up straight away.

'We're here, Davy boy.' Silas smiled; it was the first time he had, since Beth had peppered him with questions as they'd churned up the miles on the M6. Signs to the Lakes District and the Yorkshire Dales had fuelled Beth's desire to see as much of the country as she could

The trip up had started out pleasantly enough. Silas hadn't talked much, and once he'd responded to her early questions about their route he'd concentrated on his driving.

Beth had pulled the journal from her handbag, and spent a few hours reading, only putting it aside on the three occasions they'd stopped to stretch their legs and have something to eat.

On the last leg of the trip, he'd nodded at the journal.

'What're you reading?'

Beth looked up with a smile as he glanced across at her. 'You know, I'm not really sure. My great-aunt left a trunk full of journals in the house. And they've been there since she passed on.'

'So what aren't you sure about?'

She looked up at him and his gaze was sharp.

She closed the journal on her lap and shrugged. 'Whether they were stories she made up or a true chronicle of her travels. Or a combination.'

'What makes you wonder that?'

'Alice seemed to travel to a lot of places. The problem is, apart from in this one'—she held the leather-bound book up—'there are no dates and very few place names in her writing. It's really hard to figure out the sequence of the books, and where she actually is writing about.'

Silas shook his head and turned his attention back to the road as they passed through a small village on the Scottish border just after Carlisle. 'So why do you need to know? Why are you even reading them?'

She chuckled. 'First off, it's family. And then I'm a historian. I thought I might have discovered a wealth of primary observations.'

'Primary?'

'Yes actual accounts of a certain time by an observer who was there. Alice seems to have written these diaries over her entire life. She died in 2008, and was well into her eighties, so her journals would cover much of last century. I've already read about how she was a land girl in the Second World War. '

This time it was Silas who chuckled. 'Was she? Good old Alice. I'm not surprised.'

Beth narrowed her gaze. 'You sound as though you knew her?'

'I met her a couple of times.'

'So you've been friends with David for a long time? She died over ten years ago.' She looked at him. He didn't look much more than thirty. 'Did David's family live in the cottage when he was a teenager? Did you both grow up in Pilton?'

Silas seemed flustered and lifted one hand from the wheel to run it through his hair. His hair was dark, and she'd noticed a strand of grey in it when they'd stood in the sun having a coffee at a service centre during their second stop in the early afternoon.

'Ah, lots of questions. What shall I answer first?'

'Where did you grow up?'

'I grew up in Ireland.'

'When did you meet David? Before the band? I don't really know much about him. I've avoided reading any rock star gossip, and I suppose I do seem like a sticky beak, but I'm interested in finding out what I can about my family.'

'We met at art college together in London in our late teens. He must have brought me down to the family cottage then, and that's when I met your aunt. I really can't remember. You know, the haze of teenage years?' His tone was evasive and he kept his eyes ahead.

Beth shook her head but didn't argue. She could remember her teenage years very well. Her time at high school, her friends, where she'd been and the trip to the cottage when she was about to start university. Each memory was clear to her and etched into her memory. 'Yes, I suppose. So the cottage belonged to David's family?'

'Look, I really don't know. If you're curious, you'll have to ask David.' And that had been the end of the discussion. They hadn't talked much after that.

As they waited, the lights of a boat came around the edge of the point where the castle was lit up and moved quickly towards them.

'You stay in the car. It'll be monkeys outside.' Silas went to open the door but Beth put her hand on his arm.

'What? Monkeys?

'Yeah, bloody cold enough to freeze them off. You know? Brass monkeys? Or isn't it cold enough down under to use that expression?'

'Oh, yes. I get it now. I'm more used to hearing the entire phrase.'

'Anyway, whatever. You wait here till the boat gets to the shore. There's a small pier on the other side of the gatehouse. I'll get your bag.'

'Leave my dress. I'll get that.'

It was only a few minutes before the boat disappeared behind the small brick building.

As Beth opened the car door to climb out, David appeared with a flashlight. He held the door as she got out of the Land Rover before reaching over and kissing her cheek.

'Welcome to Scotland, Beth. Megan's so excited about you being here. I really appreciate you making the trip over. She doesn't have many friends here yet.

'It was good of you to invite me. And to get Silas to bring me up was very kind. I could have caught the train.'

David's grin was wide and in the bright moonlight, Beth could see the happiness in his dark eyes. 'Slim was going stir crazy here with all the wedding preparations. Did him a favour, didn't it, man?'

'Yep. Not a problem.'

'I hope he wasn't too boring a driver. Slim can be quiet when he's off stage.'

'The trip was good.' Beth turned to Silas. 'Thank you, Silas. Or should I call you Slim?'

'Either or. I answer to both.' He seemed even more distant now that they had arrived.

Beth hoisted her handbag over her shoulder and opened the back door. She carefully lifted her dress out and half folded it over her arm. She would avoid Silas or Slim from now on. She got the impression he didn't enjoy her company, so that suited her just fine.

Chapter 13

Silas sat back in the leather lounge in the small living room on the top floor of the castle. He grinned; David had gone all out for this wedding, although Silas would have much preferred to be in the Bahamas, rather than freezing his balls in the middle of a Scottish loch. Although to be fair, the roaring fire in the room, and the red wine and hot pasties had warmed him up quickly.

It was a relief to be with others this evening. He'd almost blown it when he'd told Beth he'd met Alice. Trying to explain it, without letting on where and when had had him scrabbling for answers, but he thought he'd covered up okay.

'Always stick as close to the truth as you can.' That had been their mantra when he and Davy and Bear had travelled.

Silas lifted his glass and sipped as he watched Megan and her sister, Kathy, chatting to Beth.

Bear would have been in his element. It was still hard to adjust to him not being here. It was also a wake-up call; he knew he had to decide whether he was going to stay or go back.

'Aren't you, Slim?'

Silas brought himself back from his thoughts as Megan called out to him.

'Sorry I was miles away. Aren't I what?'

'A great dancer.' Megan giggled but Beth's face remained impassive. 'I was telling Beth that you and she will be the second couple up on the dance floor after us tomorrow night.'

'I wouldn't say great, but I can waltz.'

Beth finally smiled, but it was a rueful smile. 'I'm afraid I've got two left feet. I've never been much good at that sort of dancing. Too much discoing as we grew up, to learn how to dance properly.

'Oh, God yes.' Megan chuckled. 'Remember those disco nights at the surf club?'

Silas sat back and let the conversation wash over him. He watched Beth when she threw her head back and laughed. Her red hair caught the firelight, and her eyes were full of mirth. He couldn't take his eyes off her; she was beautiful.

And not only that, her conversation on the way up—before he'd put an end to the pleasant chatting had shown him that she was a sweet person too. Something unwanted stirred deep within him, but he fought it.

Beth McLaren was dangerous to his peace of mind.

The door opened and David came back in with an armful of logs. He attended to the fire before going over to the bar.

'A top up, Slim?' He held up the bottle of red wine.

'Just a small one and then I'm going to hit the sack. It's been a long day. Poor Beth had to wake me up this morning.'

As soon as the words were out of his mouth, he realised what he'd said. He looked across at Beth. A flush tinted her cheekbones and she shook her head at Megan as her friend looked from one to the other quizzically.

'Beth woke me by knocking on the cottage door, Megan. Don't jump to conclusions!' Silas rolled his eyes. 'What do you think I am? Some sort of irresistible playboy?'

He didn't like the look on Megan's face as she gave him a considering look, but he wasn't going to feed the conversation any more. After draining his glass on one gulp he pushed up out of the soft sofa. 'I'm going to bed. At least one of us will be fresh and bright for the wedding day. Night all.' He didn't look at Beth as he walked to the door; he was altogether aware of her already.

He held the door open as Tony and Kathy followed him.

'We'll go to bed too. Time to put this young man to bed,' Kathy said as she cradled Jack in her arms. 'Night, girls. See you in the morning.'

***

Beth looked down into her glass, disappointed that Silas had left them.

'I knew he would,' Megan said softly.

Beth looked up. 'Who would what?'

'Slim. Fancy you.' Megan reached across to David and took his hand. 'Don't you agree, love?'

'Megan.' David shook his head and there was a note of warning in his voice.

'How could anyone not be attracted to you, Beth?' Megan leaned forward and her eyes were bright. 'Wait until he sees you in that dress tomorrow.'

Beth kept her voice level. 'Just because you've discovered love, and are about to be married, doesn't mean the rest of us have to enter that state. And besides Silas—Slim—has already seen my dress. It was on the back seat of the car all the way up today.'

'Ah.' Megan looked like the cat that had got the cream. 'But wait until he sees you in it.'

'Okay. Change of subject time. You can be a bugger when it comes to teasing, my darling Megan.' David put his arm along the back of the sofa. 'Tell us what you've been doing down at the cottage, Beth. Were you bored? I heard you were snowed in when you arrived. Have you given any more thought to that book you said you were going to write?'

Beth shook her head. 'Until I figure out Alice's journals—a lot of it is disconnected rambling—it's hard to say. It's been confusing to read, but really interesting. I just wish she'd dated the entries. There is only one year with a date on the entries. 1971.' As she looked up, she caught a strange glance between Megan and David, and then David's brow creased as she continued. 'I meant to ask you something, David.'

'Was the David she talked about in the cottage next door related to you? She talks about a David and his two friends.'

David cleared his throat. 'Yes. An uncle. He was a songwriter too. Did she mention his friends' names?' His voice seemed overly casual and Megan was looking at her intently.

'No, she said something about the short one makes her laugh. There was no name. It was a long time ago.'

David nodded. 'Yes, it was.'

'Did you have anyone in your family called Branton?'

This time David shrugged. 'Not that I have heard of. But I didn't live in the cottage until recently. When Megan was there last year.'

'I get the impression that this Branton was the love of her life. But then she goes into fictional stories about wars and battlefields.'

'The story writing talent must be in your genes then.' David stood and held his hand out to Megan. 'Come on, sleepyhead. You need to get your beauty sleep if I'm going to marry you tomorrow.'

Megan pushed his hand away playfully, but Beth was envious of the look they shared. No one had ever looked like that. Not even Philip when he'd proposed; his face had looked more like he was proposing a merger in a board meeting, not a marriage.

But she'd found out in time, that was how he saw it.

'You go to bed, sweetheart,' Megan stood and put her arms around David's neck. 'And remember you're sleeping in with Silas. You don't get to see me until the service tomorrow.'

Beth looked into the fire as they shared a lingering kiss, and David's hands dropped to cup Megan's behind. A strange feeling ran through her as she imagined what it would be like to be held like that by Silas. He had the most beautiful hands, she thought with a shiver.

Her gaze settled on the blue flames as David walked Megan to the door where they shared another kiss, as he murmured to Megan. It was hard to push the envy away.

Not only was David a fine-looking man, he was a good person, a talented musician, and wealthy to boot.

Megan was one lucky woman.

Beth looked up at her friend as David closed the door behind him. Her cheeks were rosy, her eyes were bright and a happy smile tilted her lips. 'I was just thinking what a lucky woman you are,' she said.

Megan sat on the sofa beside her. 'I am.' She reached out and took Beth's hand. 'It's so good to have you here. It's just a shame that we're going on our honeymoon and we won't have much time to spend together.'

'I'll still be here for a few months. And who knows where I'll travel to next. I seriously don't think that I'll go back to Sydney. I know I've hardly been here, but it just feels right. I feel like I've come home.'

'Even in that ancient cottage, with the creaky floorboards and the noisy taps? And sometimes the water stops working when— '

Beth shook her head. 'I know it's only been a few days, but seriously Megs, when I was here ten years ago, I felt it then too. The cottage has been in our family for a couple of hundred years—I'm going to find out how long. It must be genetic memory or something.'

'So how long do you think you'll stay there?' Meg dropped her gaze to their joined hands and she squeezed Beth's fingers.

'I'd like to see a whole year out. I can afford it. It'll let me see all the seasons, and give me time to explore the area, and look up all the church records. I'm determined to get to the bottom of these stories.

The more I read them, the more convinced I am that it is Alice's life.

'You mightn't like what I'm going to say, but I'm your friend and it needs to be said.'

Beth looked at Megan. She had closed her eyes and her mouth was tight. 'What needs to be said?'

'Are you sure this isn't a reaction to what Phillip did to you? That you've run away and you're looking for something to fill that gap.'

'Okay, I'll be honest. He's the reason that Sydney holds no appeal for me. At the university there's always the chance of running into him—and her—but Megs, it's not just that. Yeah okay, he did a number on me, and he fed my low self-esteem. Whatever I did, whatever I said, whatever I wore, was never good enough for him. It was constant criticism, but then he'd tell me how much he loved me and how he couldn't live without me, and I was caught. I believed him.'

'Until you discovered the truth.'

Beth was surprised. For the first time since she'd overheard Phillip's conversation, she didn't feel upset thinking or talking about it.

'Yeah, it's not nice to know that you're 'loved' because someone values your family money and flash house on the harbour more than they think of you. I had a close call.'

'Did you ever tell Phillip that you overheard him talking to Cherie?'

Beth grinned; really, it wasn't hurting any more. She thought about it in the same way you probe a sore tooth and she was pleased when the usual pain and self-confidence plunge didn't come arrowing in. Maybe she was getting over it.

'No. I bided my time. I simply waited until the next time that he did something that had been bugging me for ages. It was quite funny actually.' Now that she could look back on what had happened without being brought undone by it, Beth could see the funny side of it.

'What happened?'

'We were at the Opera House bar about a week before the wedding and we'd ordered dinner. As soon as I gave my order to the waitress, Phillip looked at me and shook his head. 'You really shouldn't have ordered that,' he said. And then he actually called the waiter back and changed my order. "She doesn't want that," he said. He didn't even look at me! I sat there and looked back at him for a minute without saying a word. He stared back looking smug and supercilious. I pulled my engagement ring off and said maybe Cherie would like this. Maybe she knows what to order in a restaurant, you dickhead.' Beth let a chuckle escape. 'And then I stood up and picked up his beer and poured it over his head. The look of horror on his face confirmed it for me. He cared nothing about me; it was what he could get out of being married to the daughter of the vice-chancellor. One night he'd even talked about the great inheritance I'd get one day! I was so naïve. Never again!'

'I guess he didn't know when he said that your father was about to leave and start a new family.'

'No, poor Mum. You know, as much as she criticised me for coming over here, I do worry about her. She's drinking too much and she's lonely.' Beth reached for her glass. 'Anyway, girlfriend, this isn't what we should be talking about on the eve of your wedding.' She lifted her wine in a toast. 'This is a special wish from me that you'll always be happy with your 'Davy' as Silas calls him. I mean it, Megs. I think you've found a man who will love you for a lifetime and I wish you every happiness in the world.' She put the glass on the table and leaned over and hugged her best friend.

'I want the same for you, Bethie.' After a moment Megan leaned back and wiped the tears from her eyes. 'I want to see you as happy as I am.'

Beth shook her head sadly. 'Not for me, sweets. Not after what Philip did, and what I saw Dad do to Mum. I will never trust a man again. I'm content with where I am in life.'

Chapter 14

Beth had to hold back her tears on more than one occasion the next afternoon. Their morning had been spent in the company of hairdressers and makeup artists who had come up from Edinburgh. The hours flew past and it wasn't long before she and Megan were walking down the stone staircase clutching their bouquets.

'Nervous?" Beth shot a glance at her friend but Megan shook her head.

'No, just happy to be getting married finally. I love David so much, there's no nerves.'

The wedding was beautiful, and an emotional occasion. Feeling very honoured to be a part of it, Beth vowed she wouldn't cry; the day was Megan's. Her friend looked stunning in her full-length lace wedding dress, with a train that stretched out like one a princess would wear. A delicately embroidered veil covered the length of the train that trailed three metres behind Megan as she walked down the aisle.

David was equally gorgeous in a pale grey suit. His white shirt had a ruffled front and cuffs. But it was the smile on his face that got everyone's attention.

And so was Silas.

Gorgeous, that was.

Beth stared as she preceded Megan down the aisle toward the two handsome men waiting at the front of the Great Hall. She still couldn't think of Silas as Slim. The two men looked like they were from the seventies; she knew it was an era that they were comfortable with as a lot of the music they played was from those years.

The service was short, but full of love. The guests smiled and nodded as the vows were repeated. The look on David's face as he took Megan's hand spoke volumes. Never before had Beth seen love like that in a man's expression. Never for her, or for anyone else. Tears prickled at the back of her eyes and she blinked.

She lasted until the end of the service; Beth couldn't hold back the tears when David's voice filled the hall as Silas handed him his guitar and he stood in front of Megan.

'*For Megan*,' he said simply.

Beth had heard the song before and loved it, so she knew David had changed the words to suit the occasion as he sang:

'You came back to me, I found you.

I love you, I love you.

Forever.'

The notes hovered in the air and Beth reached up to wipe her tears away as David put the guitar aside and reached for Megan. He held her face in his hands for a full minute before he lowered his head and took her lips with his. Beth was close enough to hear his words of love as he spoke to Megan.

Her hands shook and she gripped the bouquet tightly. *Oh to be loved like that.* It was a rare thing to see. The celebrant proclaimed them man and wife and Beth smiled through her tears. Many of the guests laughed when David stepped back, his grin wide, as he yelled, 'Let's get this party started, baby!'

Megan put her arm through David's and they headed through the crowd towards the Great Hall where the reception was being held. Beth stood back and jumped when a warm hand settled on her waist.

'Are you okay, Beth?'

She'd forgotten the best man. Silas's head dipped close to hers and she could smell the woodsy aftershave coming from his skin. It was enticing, but she pulled back a little.

'I am.' She smiled up at him. 'I'm just so happy for them, I couldn't stop the tears. Happy tears.'

He smiled back and lifted his broad shoulders in a gentle shrug. 'I guess it must be a woman thing. I just want to celebrate with them. But I'm happy for them too. I've never seen Davy so content and settled in all the time I've known him. Come on, let's go into the reception.' He held her gaze and warmth suffused her chest as he crooked his arm. 'I'll do my best man duties, and look after the bridesmaid, and then can I get you a champagne?'

The wait staff were already circulating in the cavernous hall with trays of champagne as David and Megan moved through the guests thanking them for coming. Two fires burned in the huge fireplaces at each end of the large space and Silas led Beth over to the brick wall between the fireplace and a small window seat tucked beneath the mullioned window. Soft cushions covered with bright woollen rugs filled the space.

'Thank you. A drink would be good.'

Silas dropped his hand, but before he walked away, he leaned in closer so Beth could hear him over the hubbub of the conversations filling the hall. 'I haven't told you yet. You look absolutely stunning today.'

The warmth spread up her neck and into her cheeks. Maybe it wasn't the room temperature that was making her feel hot. 'Thank you. It's a special dress.' She tried to take the seriousness from the moment with a smile. 'It was worth the hassle of bringing it all the way from Australia.'

'You could be the lady of the castle. You look like someone from medieval days. That thing on your hair finishes it off perfectly.'

Megan had found an emerald green hair filet and hadn't told Beth until they were getting dressed.

The hairdresser had braided Beth's hair before the ceremony and wound the braids around the crown of her head before covering the sides with the emerald green velvet hair piece that Megan pulled from her bag.

Now she reached up self-consciously and touched her braids.

Silas held her gaze a moment longer before Beth dropped her eyes. He headed off to chase down one of the waiters. She watched thoughtfully as he walked away, noticing the appreciative glances from the women he passed.

His wedding suit fitted him perfectly and showed off his lean muscled body. The grey trousers were snug on his thighs as he moved through the crowd. His jet-black hair was pulled back with a leather tie accentuating his strong jaw and full lips.

Beth took a deep breath. Why on earth were her thoughts focused on Silas? Heat rolled over her, and warmed her blood.

This was crazy. Almost surreal.

As the man in her thoughts walked back towards her carrying two glasses of champagne Beth firmed her resolve. It was time to get her act together.

She was way past the age for falling for someone just because of good looks and a sexy voice. Someone who knew how to breach her barriers by throwing a few compliments her way.

Gosh, I get sucked in. Think of Phillip, she chastised herself. And besides, she had to remember the hard lesson she'd learned; she wasn't falling for anyone ever again. Even if they were extra good looking, kind and showing interest in her.

So her response to Silas as he stood close and held out the glass of champagne may have been extra cool. He could deal with it and go and find someone else to chat up. One more night here and she could retreat to the cottage and immerse herself in the diaries again.

Beth stood there quietly sipping her drink, but Silas didn't take the hint as she looked away from him. Finally she couldn't help herself.

'Ah, Silas? Just because you drove me up here, please don't feel you have to entertain me. I'm quite happy being alone and enjoying the atmosphere of the castle. I don't need company.' She tried to keep her tone polite but it obviously came out short and brusque because his eyes narrowed.

'So should I take that as a brush-off?'

'No. Of course not.' Beth stumbled over her words. 'I just didn't want you to feel as though you had to ignore your friends and keep me company.'

A slow grin spread over his face and God help her, she couldn't take her eyes from his face. Their gazes collided and held, and Beth was the first one to look away.

Reluctantly.

Warm pressure on her wrist had her looking down. Silas's long fingers encircled her wrist.

'Friends? What makes you think I know all of these people? They're David's and Megan's. I'm simply a guitarist who flits in and out of Davy's sessions now and then.'

Beth frowned. 'But I thought you were in his band?'

'I was once, but not anymore. It's complicated now.' Silas's fingers brushed her skin as he spoke. 'I'm here with you because I enjoy your company, no other reason. And I would like to get to know you better.'

'Oh.' Beth felt silly. She couldn't think of anything gracious to say in response. She wasn't sure if she wanted to get to know him any better. It would simply make him more attractive to her, and she didn't need that the way she was feeling.

'Come on. Let's go and get something to eat and we'll sit down and people watch. I'll point out some of the big "names" who are here. That's if you're interested.'

Before she could protest—not that she really wanted to, to be honest— Silas was leading her over to a huge buffet table filled with a selection of food. He passed her a fine china white plate and stepped back to let her choose what she wanted.

Beth was getting more nervous by the minute; her appetite had fled. She chose a couple of small hors d'oeuvres and put them on her plate before moving across to a double seat beneath a large window. She was way too aware of Silas, and after what he'd said about wanting to get to know her better, her nerves were running wild. She'd never been very comfortable in social situations, and since she'd started going out with Phillip she had always been able to fade into the background. Phillip had loved being in the limelight, talking to the people who mattered.

Or those that he thought mattered.

If it had been up to her, she would have preferred quiet nights out together, but Phillip always liked to be "seen". As Beth sat there waiting for Silas to come back, she closed her eyes. She could recall vividly the frustration of being with her ex. The relationship had been different for want of a better word; he thought it was good for her to get out socially.

It had taken that overheard conversation to make her realise how foolish she'd been.

Her preference had been to stay in, with occasional quiet conversation, and an intimate dinner with her partner, but it had seemed that when they did that, they would run out of conversation early in the night. She would end up reading happily, and depending on the season Phillip would watch the football or the cricket before he went home. Sometimes she'd wondered if he was the man for her, and then they'd go out, and she'd see him holding court, and being witty, and entertaining, and she would be content. Thank goodness they hadn't moved in together, even after they got engaged.

If she hadn't overheard that conversation that had been the catalyst for her breaking the engagement, she probably would have married Phillip. Was she so naïve that her feelings could change so quickly?

It hadn't been love; she didn't know what that felt like, but one thing she did know, with Phillip— or anyone else—she'd never experienced this wild feeling that ran through her blood every time Silas stood near her. It made her feel alive.

She would *not* trust the feeling, no matter how good it made her feel. The excitement and anticipation that licked at her nerve endings was unfamiliar, but . . . maybe . . .

No. It could be dangerous.

It would be foolish.

But it could be fun, a little voice nagged.

Silas walked over balancing a plate of food, and flashed her a wide grin when she looked at his plate. He sat close to her and she grabbed for his plate as the food threatened to slide off.

'I'm hungry,' he said, his eyes sparkling.

The middle cushion sagged, and Beth slid down towards the gap. Her leg pressed hard against his, but because of the softness of the cushions, she couldn't move back to the edge of the sofa. A little ripple of warmth shot up her thigh to places she'd rather not be involved, and Beth caught her breath.

Don't be a fool, she told herself sternly. Annoyance filled her; she should have learned her lesson.

That little voice again. *Why hesitate? Give me one good reason why you couldn't indulge in a little* fun while you're here in this fabulous castle. A gorgeous man, no commitment on either side. Just fun.

She bit her lip and smoothed her hand down the soft green velvet of her dress. When she looked up, Silas's eyes were on her, and heat ran up her neck when he smiled.

'You were,' she said nodding at his plate. 'Um, hungry I mean.'

When she'd walked down the aisle ahead of Megan this afternoon, both Silas and David had smiled. David's smile had been happy and friendly, Silas's had been enough to make her knees tremble; she knew then she had to stay away from him. Now that same smile held intimacy.

God.

She swallowed.

Self-confidence, girl. Beth lifted her chin and held his gaze. She was a grown woman, not far off thirty. The years were flying by.

And she *wanted* to be foolish. Even if only for this wedding weekend up in Scotland. She had months ahead of her to be the staid academic historian and reader of journals.

Time is fleeting. Seize each opportunity. Make the most of every minute.

Alice had repeated those three sentences in her journals. Every journal that Beth had read so far had those words somewhere there in the pages. The words chanted in her head like a mantra.

Okay, she could get her confidence up.

I can do it. Beth knew she could make the most of this opportunity. He was attracted to her, and she was to him. She lifted her eyes and her resolve firmed.

'That's an interesting smile. A real Mona Lisa smile.' His voice was low and he leaned over close so she could hear him. 'You're a thinker, aren't you, Beth? His warm breath brushed her ear, and sent a shiver coursing down her back.

'Goes with the territory,' she replied. 'I'm a historian. I can't help analysing situations.'

'What are you thinking about now?'

Her lips tilted upwards a little further. 'If you're good, I might tell you later.'

His eyes widened as she flirted with him, and common sense disappeared like the melting snowflakes as they touched the warm glass beside them.

'Oh, I can be good.'

'Not the bad rock star image then?'

His chuckle brought that shiver back. 'I tried it once, but it didn't work for me. Give me a quiet life any day.'

Beth nodded. 'That's my preference too.' Her days would be quiet enough when she went back to the cottage. For these two days and nights, she'd smile at Silas, and talk to him, and dance with him. And whatever came of tonight she would accept.

Time is fleeting. Seize each opportunity. Make the most of every minute.

And she would be confident as she did it. Excitement rippled through her. Her future was unknown, and so was this weekend.

Silas gestured to her plate. 'That wouldn't feed a sparrow.'

'I wasn't hungry. Too nervous, I guess.'

'Well, Beth, the wedding ceremony is over. The best man and the bridesmaid are no longer required and no one is interested in you and me. The bride and groom are the centre of attention, so there's no need for nerves any more. Unless it's me making you nervous?' As he spoke he put his plate on the small table next to the sofa and reached out and took her hand.

She shook her head, but her reply was a bit too fast to be believable. 'No. No, of course not.' She gestured around the room. 'This is all out of my experience. I'm not used to being in crowds like this. And so many famous people here too apparently.'

'Don't let that intimidate you.' This time Silas shook his head. 'Fame is simply a perception. It's not real.'

Beth detected bitterness in his tone. 'It is. It's recognition we give when someone achieves something notable,' she said.

'Depends on whether what some perceive as notable is really important, and whether they let it go to their head. I've seen too many bad things in my life to be comfortable with fame. Like I said, it's the quiet life for me.' He let go of her hand and picked up an oyster from his plate. As he tilted his head back Beth watched his eyes close as he savoured the taste.

'If someone has a true talent, they can be admired for it,' she persisted. Silas's reaction was interesting and she'd learned more about him in the last few minutes than she had in the whole long trip north.

'Okay, we all have a talent, so should we all be famous?' He leaned back against the sofa. 'In this century, it's gone crazy. Superstardom, celebrities. I can't handle it.' He lowered his voice again. 'Sorry, I've jumped on my bandwagon there. Forget I said anything. It's a pet peeve of mine. Often those who think they are most deserving of adulation, are the least worthy.' He shook his head and reached back and toyed with the leather band on his hair. 'Enough of this. We're here to celebrate. So to get back to where we began, there's no need to be nervous. You look gorgeous, you could hold your own, and more, with any one of these so called celebrities, so let's just sit back and have fun.'

Beth picked up her champagne and sipped, unable to think of anything more she could say. Silas was an enigma, and his ideas were different. It was going to be an interesting weekend.

***

Silas walked back from the bar with two glasses of champagne; the toasts and speeches were about to begin. The pale sun glowed through the window and created a halo effect around Beth's head. She looked so damn perfect sitting on the window seat in the alcove; she could have been from the fifteenth century. Her skin was almost translucent and she'd done something to her eyes that made them turn up at the corners, giving her a mysterious look. Her glorious red hair was pulled back in a braid circle, revealing the exquisite shape of her face that had been hidden yesterday when her hair was loose and around her face.

Yesterday in the car, he'd sensed she was shy, and that her self-confidence had taken a beating some time. Megan had mentioned a past relationship that had left Beth fragile, and he found himself wanting to reassure her. The complication was that he was going to be living next door to her in David's cottage for as long as she was there reading Alice's journals.

The content of the journals was an unknown, and both Megan and David were terrified that she'd outlined how to get through the stones. He'd committed to keeping Beth safe while ever she was living in the cottage.

She was staring out at the snow. It was getting dark and soon there'd be no reason for her to look out of the window. Silas knew she was avoiding his gaze as he approached, and he was wondering whether the flirtatious banter had been wise.

He'd had too many one-night stands and Beth was better than that. The problem was he found her too damn beautiful and all he could think of was taking her to his bed.

He would pull back, or it would do his head in.

'Here you are, milady,' he said with a smile as handed her the glass. Their fingers brushed and he noticed how she quickly pulled her hand back.

'Thank you.'

Most of the guests had found somewhere to sit, and they had a good view of the raised dais in the middle of the hall where Megan and Davy now stood.

'Are you happy to stay here or do you want to move closer? There's a spare table at the edge of the dance floor.'

'This is fine,' she said softly as Davy took the microphone. Silas sat at the end of the window seat in the opposite corner to Beth.

It didn't work though; he was just as aware of her when she sat further away from him. At least she was too far away for him to reach out and touch her, like he wanted to.

Needed to.

God, what was wrong with him? He'd never been so enamoured of a woman before. He wanted her and the feeling was sharp and persistent.

Trust me, he wanted to say.

'Welcome everyone.' The mike crackled as Davy stood on the dais with his arm around Megan's waist. 'Thank you for coming to celebrate with us today. I know some of you have come a very long way to share our day with us.' He looked over at Silas and winked.

Davy's hidden meaning pulled Silas's thoughts back to the wedding, and he relaxed as he listened to the speeches. He even managed not to look at Beth for a full five minutes. The formalities were short and amusing, and as Davy wound up, he looked over at Silas and Beth.

'I'm going to invite my best man, Slim Rogers, and Megan's bridesmaid, the beautiful Beth

McLaren, to join us on the dance floor for the bridal waltz.' Davy chuckled. 'Hey, Slim, it'll take the pressure off me. I might be able to play guitar, but I'm no dancer.'

Silas stood and held his hand out to Beth. 'Looks like we've got one more job to do.'

She smiled sweetly and his heart gave a little jolt in his chest.

Hand-in-hand, they walked over to the dance floor as the sad notes of the piano came from the speakers and Joe Cocker's voice rasped out the first line of *You are So Beautiful.*

Davy and Megan smiled at them as Silas held his arms out and Beth stepped into them. He drew in a deep breath as he put his hand around her waist and held her close. Close but not too close, but she fitted in his arms perfectly. Beth's hand trembled in his and Silas whispered close to her ear. 'Don't be nervous, I can lead.'

Beth leaned back to look up at him, her eyes wide. 'I can dance,' she whispered back. 'It's the crowd watching every step that makes me nervous.'

Silas lowered his head and her breath brushed his cheek as she opened her mouth to speak. He shook his head. 'It's okay, they'll all be on the dance floor after this song finishes.' He pulled her close again and this time their bodies touched, and he strangled back a groan. Beth's breasts were soft against his chest for a fleeting second, but the softness was imprinted on his memory. The soft velvet of her dress was smooth and sensuous against the hand that he kept carefully at her waist. Her other hand was cradled in his as they took the first steps to glide across the dance floor.

They were perfect together; he had known they would be. As they waltzed, Beth moved closer until Silas imagined he could feel her heart beating in time to their steps. Slow and heavy, filled with promise.

Beth responded to his every movement, in sync with his steps. He looked down at her and their gazes locked and held as they danced.

'You're everything I need.' The music flowed around them, and he spread his fingers across her lower back. He held his breath when Beth moved her head closer to his. Silas leaned down and closed his eyes as he rested his cheek against hers.

He felt her smile against his skin and he was lost as an acute surge of desire engulfed him.

***

Beth could have stayed in Silas's arms all night. The bridal waltz had long finished, and most of the other guests were on the dance floor with them. Despite the crowd around them, Silas led her effortlessly and she followed his lead as the gentle pressure of his hand on her back guided her. Her blood thrummed in her veins in time with her heart beat, slow and heavy; her limbs were fluid and loose. Yearning flared, and Silas must have sensed it, because he pulled her closer. His chest was hard against her, and his fingers on her back were sending need spiralling to her lower belly. Her thighs clenched as his hand followed the curve of her back.

Lower and lower.

It was as though they were one, there was only one way they could be closer, and Beth knew that was inevitable before the night was over. She pulled her head back as anticipation coursed through her. Blue eyes held hers, and a sexy smile tilted his lips. Beth let go of his hand and reached up to encircle both arms around his neck.

As Silas's lips settled in the hollow of her neck Beth let out a gentle sigh as quiet sensuality consumed her.

'You're beautiful, Beth.' It was the first words that he had spoken since they had begun the waltz, four or five songs ago. She'd lost track of time as she'd relished being held. She knew her eyes were dazed as she lifted her head and stared at him.

'I feel beautiful.' Her heart wasn't beating that slow rhythm now; it felt as though it was about to burst out of her chest.

He lowered his head and Beth caught her breath as his lips slid up her neck, and then up her cheek before stopping at the edge of her mouth.

The wait was unbearable so she turned her head slightly and his mouth took hers. No longer gentle, she could sense his need; it was fierce and urgent.

Her fingers tangled in his hair and she pushed against him.

The tempo of the music changed, startling her out of the world she was lost in.

Pausing, she missed a step as she put her hand to her hot cheeks and stared at Silas. His eyes mirrored hers, slumberous and full of need. He quirked an eyebrow, waiting for her to speak.

There was only one thing she could say.

'My room or yours?'

Chapter 15

Beth could have stayed in the castle for the rest of her life quite happily. In the early hours of the morning after the wedding, she woke in Silas's arms. Few words had been spoken after he'd led her up the stone staircase to his room and gently peeled the green velvet dress from a woman who was willing.

She had taken her pleasure slowly undoing the buttons beneath the ruffles of his shirt, pausing occasionally to run her fingers over the silken skin of his chest.

Now, in the breaking dawn fingers of pale light began to illuminate the massive bedroom, and she nestled against his warm body listening to him breathe quietly beside her. Her body still tingled and an incredible sense of wellbeing and mellowness enveloped her as he slept on.

And confidence. Confident that she had followed her heart and not her common sense for a change. A smile lifted her lips as she turned to the sleeping man beside her. A surge of unfamiliar feeling filled her chest and her eyes pricked from the intensity of the emotion as it ran through he.

Silas was a skilful and considerate lover and she'd felt more cherished than she ever had in her life. In the midst of a raging kiss, he'd paused and asked her if she was sure, and she had even wondered briefly if he was as keen as she was.

Beth smiled as she lifted her hand and ran it down his chest . . . she had to touch him; it was impossible to lie there and not put her hands on him. His skin was like satin, and warm and—

Firm fingers held hers and she looked up to a pair of smiling, sexy eyes.

'If you do that you'll end up in trouble.' The husky voice sent a shiver down to those parts of her that were still tingling after a couple of hours of sleep.

'Was that trouble we had before? Three times trouble?' A giggle escaped her lips as he held her hand steady, away from the destination she'd been heading for. 'I've never been in trouble before, but I must say I quite liked it.'

'So you're one of those good girls I've heard about then, I guess,' Silas teased before he let go of her hand. He pushed himself up in the bed and leaned his head against the ornate timber bedhead and held up his arm so she could snuggle against him. 'But I'm pleased to hear that.' He leaned across and dropped a kiss on the top of her head and warmth suffused her. There was nothing sexual about it, just sheer affection, and Beth closed her eyes. There was no self-consciousness about being in his bed; no angst about what she would say or do.

'Has anyone ever told you what beautiful hands you have?'

He picked up her hand again and examined her fingers in the half light. He held it high in front of them. 'You have the fingers of a musician. Have you ever played an instrument?'

She nodded. 'I played acoustic guitar until my ex complained.'

'You did? Why the hell would anyone complain about that?'

'Long story. It wasn't seen to be the trendy thing. And this isn't the right place or time to talk about it. Needless to say I don't play anymore.'

Regret shot through her as she thought of what else she'd given up for Phillip.

'You could take it up again.'

'Maybe. But I'm pretty busy for a while with the journals. I've set a goal.'

'Beth?'

'Mm?'

'I need to tell you something. You need to know.''

Her eyes flew open and her body stiffened. *Oh, please don't tell me that I was kidding myself. And that last night was a mistake.*

'Yes?' she said slowly, already distancing herself from him. *Emotionally and mentally.*

Moving away physically was impossible; Silas must have sensed her withdrawal because his arm was like a steel vice across her shoulder.

'Don't stress. I'm hoping it's good news.' He tucked his chin on the top of her head and she waited. 'When I take you back to Somerset, I'm going to be staying in Davy's cottage for a while. I just don't want you to think I'm stalking you or anything after last night. I talked it over with him the other night.'

Joy coursed through her; she'd thought this dalliance was only for the weekend of the wedding. Sense came zooming in fast. 'So, tell me why?'

Another pause had unease bubbling up into her chest, and her confidence disappearing quickly. She tried to move away but he held her fast.

'Uh uh.' He shook his head. 'Don't take it the wrong way. I was worried that you would think it was merely because of last night.'

'Last night?' Her voice was hesitant now and she relaxed as his voice softened.

'Oh, Beth, don't think like that.'

'Like what?' This time she managed to twist away from his grip, and she pulled the sheet up to cover her bare breasts, suddenly feeling self-conscious.

'Oh fuck it. Listen to me, Beth. I'm not good with words. Shit, I can write love songs, but when it comes to my own life . . . '

'Yes?' Her voice was prim. She'd been here before.

'I can't explain how I feel. I've never been able to, but I wanted you to know that me staying next door to you had already been arranged and has nothing to do with us getting together last night. I didn't want you to think that I was coming down to Somerset just to sleep with you. There, I've said it.'

'So why are you coming there?'

Beth sensed a hesitation but then Silas hurried to answer. 'I'm writing some songs for an album that Davy and I are going to collaborate on, and Davy suggested that his cottage would be a quiet place for me to focus on my song writing. You being there is a bonus.'

'Okay. So we can be neighbours.'

'No. After last night, it's a double bonus for me. I want you to know that what we shared was very special. No matter what the rumours are about our lifestyle and groupies and all that shit, it's not true for me.'

Beth relaxed and let him pull her close again.

'I want to get to know you Beth. I want to see what you love to do. I want to show you around. I want to spent time with you. What do you think about that?'

Beth let Silas wait for at least thirty seconds before she smiled up at him.

'I think I could get to like that very much.'

Chapter 16

A week later.

Despite the cold, it hadn't snowed in Somerset since Beth and Silas had come back to the cottages. The ground was wet sludge beneath their feet as they walked along the road to the village each morning.

They'd settled into a routine; each of them slept in their own cottage, but Rose and Violet Cottages might as well have been the same house the rest of the time. They shared everything except for a bed to sleep in at nights, although each afternoon usually found them in a bed in one of the cottages, and it wasn't for an afternoon nap.

Silas cooked dinner while Beth read, and she took coffee over to him when she heard a break in the guitar chords coming through the trees that were bare of leaves.

As crazy as it seemed, Beth knew she was falling in love with him, despite only having known him for eight days. No—correct that—she was already in love. The feeling was so powerful she recognised and accepted it for what it was.

Most importantly she trusted Silas; he was concerned for her welfare and Beth was surprised by how much he went out of his way to make sure she was content.

On the Friday morning, six days after the wedding, Silas tapped on the front door early and she dragged herself out of bed to hurry over and let him in.

'Morning, milady,' he said as he wrapped his arms around her. 'We've run out of eggs and I was going to cook you my special omelette. Fancy a walk to the village store a bit earlier today?'

'Sounds like a plan.' She stood on her toes and kissed him and a fresh soapy fragrance surrounded her. 'Mm, you smell nice.'

'I was so cold when I woke up I had a long hot shower.'

Beth looked up at him from beneath her eyelashes as he came inside and closed the door. 'Perhaps you'd be warmer sharing a bed over here tonight?'

Silas took her hand and didn't speak for a while. Beth swallowed, fearing that she'd said the wrong thing.

Eventually he lifted her hand to his lips. 'I'd like nothing better. But Beth?'

'Yes?' She held his gaze.

'I don't want you to think that I'm rushing you.'

'I know what I feel and I know what I want, Silas. I've waited a long time to feel like this. I know what this is.'

He reached out and slid his arms around her waist and dropped his chin on the top of her head. 'I first saw you a week ago today. In your pink fluffy dressing gown and fluffy socks, and your nose red from the cold.'

'It wasn't the cold. I'd been crying over Aunt Alice's diary,' Beth said indignantly.

'Whatever it was, I fell in love with you on the spot. That's why I wouldn't come inside. It scared the life out of me.'

Beth caught her breath and closed her eyes as she processed what he'd said.

'You fell in love with me?' she said slowly.

'I know. It sounds crazy doesn't it. We've known each other eight days, but I knew in that instant. You read about it, and laugh, but when it happens you know what it is. I'm sorry, Beth, I didn't want you to think I was a mad stalker or anything. I wasn't going to say it, in case I scared you.'

'You're the rock star. I would be the stalker.'

He shook his head and smiled. 'Never.'

Beth trembled in his arms as she smiled back at him. His blue eyes held hers, and reason tumbled into oblivion as she reached up and cupped his face between her hands. 'I love you too, Silas. As crazy as it sounds. I do.'

She pulled his head down so that her lips met his. The kiss was different. Soft and slow and full of promise.'

'So what are we going to do about it?' he murmured against her mouth.

Beth sighed. 'I don't know. That frightens me. I've been on this high since the night in Rothmore Castle when you took me to your bed. I don't know what it will feel like when that leaves me. I know we can't stay here forever.' Her voice hitched. 'Feeling like this has helped me to understand Alice's diary so much more this week. The emotion that she wrote about when she left Branton, and when she lost their baby.

Silas stiffened against her. 'Who was Branton?'

Beth shrugged, wondering at the intensity of his tone. 'I don't know. There was only the one entry about him so far. I think it was in the war. The only other time she mentioned him briefly she said she went back to visit him, and there seemed to be soldiers there. I know she was in the Land Army in the Second World War.'

'She went back to visit him?'

'Yes, why?' Beth looked up but Silas was staring ahead and not looking at her. His arms dropped and she sensed his withdrawal.

'Are you really getting anything out of reading those old journals. Do you really think it's worth the time you spend reading them? Is it worth how much they've upset you a couple of times?'

It was as though a door slammed in her face. Beth turned away and crossed to the window. She held back the tears that threatened. First Mum, and then Megan and Davy, and now Silas. Maybe it was time to think about why she had such a compulsion to read these diaries. Why they held such a fascination for her.

He followed her over to the window and put a tentative hand on her shoulder. 'I'm sorry. I didn't mean to upset you.'

She shook her head. 'It's not just you. It's even hard for me to understand why they're important to me. It might sound silly but it's as though Alice is trying to tell me something from the grave.'

Beth was surprised when Silas groaned. She turned around to face him, and he rubbed at his face. His gaze was intense and his eyes bored into hers.

'I know what you are saying and believe me, as hard as it may be I do understand.' He reached out for her and she stepped in and nestled against his hard chest. Contentment filled Beth and she felt safe again. For a few minutes she thought she'd put whatever it was between them at risk. He lifted his hand to move a loose strand of hair from her cheek and his voice was still intense. 'You have to listen to me, Beth. It's not a good thing to be doing.

Interfering with the past. Leave it be.' His Irish accent was more pronounced as emotion filled his voice.

'I don't understand. I'm not interfering. I'm reading Alice's stories, or diary or whatever they are. I just wish I knew. What could possibly be dangerous about that?'

But he ignored her question. 'Why don't we go away on a trip? Leave the cottages. Get to know each other. There must be other places you'd like to see? I could take you to Ireland.'

How did their conversation get to this? Confusion filled her.

'I'll just go and get changed and we'll go for that walk.' She needed to be alone for a moment to process what had just passed between them. 'We'll talk about it later.

***

Silas held Beth's hand as they walked to the village. He'd taken her the long way along the road for the past week; the one time that Beth had suggested cutting across the field near the stones, he'd avoided it by saying the ground would be wet and soft after the snow. A cool wind blew around the cottages today, and the eerie whistling sound matched his mood.

Ah Alice, what did you write in those blasted books?'

When Beth had come down dressed and ready

to go out, she'd reached up and kissed him and she seemed to be back to normal.

Whatever normal was anymore.

Silas felt like a heel, knowing that he was supposed to be here keeping her safe.

So what had he done instead? Fallen for her? Slept with her? Lied to her? All of that.

And worst—or best—knew he couldn't let her go even if it was only a week since they'd met

Jesus wept.

His life had been turned upside down by a beautiful auburn-haired woman. A woman who said she loved him back. He'd never felt like this before in his life

He felt so disloyal to Megan and Davy and afraid on two counts now. One: that he'd let them down, and the second didn't bear thinking about: that Beth would read something in those blasted journals and go exploring and get through the stones.

Oh, Alice what have you recorded?

Keeping an eye on Beth McLaren for Megan and Davy and keeping her away from the stones had sounded easy enough.

But he hadn't factored in falling for Beth and now Silas was terrified she was going to find something in the journals and go looking for the stones.

'You're quiet this morning.' Beth's soft words

interrupted his brooding as they approached the village. 'Are we okay?'

He squeezed her hand and smiled at her. 'Of course we are. I was just thinking we might forget about buying eggs and have brunch at the pub. What do you think?'

'Sounds good to me. No washing up in that old stone sink with the dodgy tap.'

They walked past the village green—not so green in the middle of winter—and past the village store. The pub had been modernised since Silas had been there last summer when he'd met Megan with Davy and it was too slick and modern for his tastes. He knew what it had been like in the seventies, and the atmosphere it had exuded.

They chose their meals from the chalk-written board, and Silas went to the bar to order a pot of tea.

'While you're ordering I'm just going to slip next door to the shop. I need a couple of things. Won't be long.' Beth hurried to the door as he waited to place the order. He watched as she went past the window at the front. Even though it wasn't snowing, it was still bloody cold and she'd pulled on thigh length leather boots over her back leggings and a full length wool coat over her olive green jumper.

Instead of grabbing a beanie, she'd worn that green head thing that she'd had on at the wedding, but this time her glorious hair flowed loose beneath it. Her cheeks were pink from their walk and as she passed by the window she waved and sent such a sweet smile in his direction his legs almost went to jelly.

How can a woman have so much impact on a man? For the first time, he understood some of the lyrics that Davy had written after he'd met Megan. And more so after he'd thought he'd lost her forever. The haunting melodies of loss and grief and the sad words had been some of their bestselling songs.

Once he'd placed their order he walked across to a table near the fireplace. His thoughts were on Alice, and how her words of loss and grief were impacting on Beth. He wondered who this Branton was: he had no doubt that the stories in Alice's journals were true. He was going to ask Beth if he could read them.

That way he could find out if she'd documented going through the stones.

Silas's phone pinged as he sat down and he pulled it from his pocket, scrolling through the messages that were there. No matter how long he stayed in this time, he still found the new-fangled cell phone intrusive. Everyone wanted an answer instantly. He scowled at the phone screen and then brightened when he saw the message was from Davy.

How goes it man? The message read. Beth still

bunkered down in her cottage? Megs thought there was something going on between you pair at the wedding and I told her not to be stupid. It was just a dance or two. She's wrong...wasn't she?

Silas's fingers hovered over the buttons, and he was tempted to tell the truth. In the end he answered simply:

All good here. Stayed away from the stones.

The reply was the thumbs ups icon. Okay, so he'd lied by omission, but whatever there was between he and Beth was no one else's business. Davy and Megan were in the Maldives on their honeymoon; they didn't need to know.

Yet.

He hoped that Jules wasn't in the village shop today. Apparently, her daughter and granddaughter ran it most of the time.

Silas had stayed away because he didn't want Jules recognising him. She was as sharp as a tack, and sure to say something to Beth.

Chapter 17

Beth had run out of shampoo and her hair was due for a wash. After they went back to the cottage, she'd wash her hair in the laundry tub and then sit by the fire with Silas and read some more while he picked at his guitar strings. She loved the routine that they were in already; she hadn't given much thought to how lonely it would have been here by herself. Even after a week of his company, she couldn't imagine him not being here with her.

Her face wore a happy smile as she pushed open the door of the village store. The bell above the door clanged and she stood for moment letting her eyes adjust to the darkness.

"Hello, luv. How was the wedding?"

Beth jumped when Jules, the shopkeeper she'd met when she'd arrived, appeared from behind the low shelves to her right. 'It was good. Went off very well.'

'That's good. I'll bet that Davy looked delicious.'

Beth smiled and simply nodded.

'What are you after today?'

'Just some shampoo please.' She followed the

woman down to the shelves near the counter and nodded when she held up a bottle of name brand shampoo.

'With hair like that, I thought you'd want the good one. Is that all today?'

'Yes, thank you. 'I can't stay. We've just ordered brunch at the pub.' She pulled out a note and handed it over, but the shopkeeper hesitated.

'We?' Her voice was curious. 'Has Alice come back to visit?'

Beth shook her head. The poor lady was as crazy as ever.

'With all those blue lights at the stones at night, I thought she must have come back.'

'Come back?' Beth said slowly as she waited for her change. 'From the dead?"

'No, silly, through the stones. Like she always did.'

'What stones?' Beth clutched the small shampoo bottle to her chest.

'The ones at the back of the cottages. Between there and Pilton Farm. They're on a magnetic line. And they're used to travel.' Jules undid her purple apron, hitched it around her huge tummy and retied the ties. 'If you don't know what you're doing, you could get lost, so you make sure you stay away from them.'

'Thank you, I will.'

Beth was preoccupied as she headed back to

the pub. Silas was quiet—there was obviously something bothering him, and she hoped it wasn't her. She got back just in time as the two meals and a pot of tea were placed on the table.

'A couple of tea cups, please Reggie.' Silas called over to the barman when the waitress didn't come back.

'Do you know that woman in the village store?' she asked Silas.

'Jules?'

'Yes, that's her.'

'I've met her a couple of times.'

'She has some crazy ideas. It amazes me that she's running a store by herself.'

'She'd been there a long time. Since the seventies.'

'She's old enough.' Beth reached for the teapot.

'Ah, yes, Davy told me she's been there forever. Or so Davy said. She must be a fair age. Um, maybe she's got dementia or something. I've heard that her family own the store now.'

'She thought you were Alice.'

'What?' Silas looked at her quizzically.

'Yes, she asked if she'd come back to visit.'

Silas swallowed. 'You did tell her that she'd passed on a few years ago?'

Beth nodded as she filled both cups with the fragrant tea. 'I did. But she started talking about blue lights, and stones.'

She glanced up at Silas and he was staring at her with a strange look on his face. His eyes were wide, and despite the cold, she could see a line of perspiration on his brow. 'What do you think she meant? She also said something about magnetic lines.'

Silas picked up his tea cup. 'Oh, that's just local lore. You haven't heard that before?' He blew on the hot tea and Beth smiled. She was getting to know his little quirks. There was nothing eccentric about him.

'It's new age stuff, probably left over from the festivals that started here in the seventies. All the hippies used to congregate here.' He put his tea down and ran a finger around the neck of his T-shirt.

'You're not getting the flu are you?' Beth asked with concern. 'You look hot.'

'No, it's just the tea making me sweat.'

'So tell me more about these lines.'

'The idea that ley lines have spiritual power or special mystical energy has been around for a long time. And it's all tied up with the legend of King Arthur and Guinevere being buried in the abbey at Glastonbury. It brings the tourists in and helps the local economy. Don't worry about Jules, she's probably been telling that story to the visitors for a long time.'

Beth looked up at the waitress who was

standing beside them with two plates.

The girl placed the meals in front of them on the table and then hovered for a moment. 'I hope you don't mind, but I couldn't help hearing what you were talking about.' She lowered her voice. 'It's true. Go over to Glastonbury town and check it out.'

'Really?' Beth frowned. 'How can you check it out?'

'There's a double line that crosses itself in three places in the town, and it creates an area that's full of energy. Some say it's a portal to time slips, but no one I know has ever been able to prove that. But if you go and stand on these spots, you get an energy message from Mother Earth.'

Silas rolled his eyes at Beth before he replied to the girl, cynicism lacing his voice. 'So what's this message? Hello, I'm Mother Earth? Is it the same for everyone?'

'There are non-believers of course, but once they stand on the crossing places, they soon change their mind. I've done it. You get an overwhelming sense of peace and balanced harmony.' The young waitress pursed her lips. 'You try it. You might get a surprise, sir.'

Beth was embarrassed by Silas's rudeness. 'Where would we find these places?' she asked.

'Well,' the girl leaned down to Beth. 'Are you just passing through or staying in Pilton or

Glastonbury?'

'We're over in the cottages across the fields. Halfway between Pilton and Glastonbury.'

'Well, you're in luck then.'

Silas picked up his knife and fork and looked pointedly at their meals. Beth shook her head. 'You start, Silas. I'm really interested in this.'

'The first place the lines cross is in the Abbey, between the High Altar and King Arthur's and Guinevere's tomb. The second place is in the High Street, but the third isn't far from here. In the fields near the stones at the back of the cottages where you're staying.'

'Beth, your meal is getting cold.' Silas's vice was cold too, and the young girl shrugged before she flounced away.

'That was interesting, wasn't it?' Beth picked up her fork and toyed with the scrambled egg on her plate. Silas's rudeness was a side she hadn't seen before, and she didn't look at him as he spoke.

'I've heard it all before, staying here,' he said with a shrug. 'Now let's talk some more about what I mentioned before.'

'What was that?' Beth's voice was chilly because she was a bit cross at him. The waitress's story had been interesting; it didn't mean that she believed it because she paid polite attention. There was no reason for Silas to be so rude. She was disappointed in him.

'Travelling together for a while. Getting away from here, and seeing more of the country. What do you think?'

She lifted her chin and stared at him. 'What do I think? I think I'm very happy to stay here and keep doing my reading and research.' She lifted her fork and pointed it at him, knowing it was bad manners. 'But if you want to go off travelling, feel quite free. There's no reason at all that you have to stay here.'

ANNIE SEATON

Chapter 18

'I'm sorry if I've upset you.' Silas reached over and took Beth's free hand. Her interest in the waitress's talk had thrown him, because he knew exactly what she'd said was true. But the girl—or Beth—didn't know the half of it.

Beth stared at him and he squeezed her fingers gently. 'I'm really sorry I was short with her. I'll apologise to the girl for my scepticism when she comes back.'

Finally Beth's fingers relaxed in his. 'And I'm sorry for snapping at you. But really, I don't want to leave the cottage yet. I'm just settling in.' She looked at him from beneath her lashes. 'And I didn't mean it about you leaving. I'd miss you if you left.'

There was no fear of that happening, he thought. 'That's good, because I'm not going to leave you.'

Now that Beth's interest in the ley lines had been piqued, and bloody hell, she knew where the stones were, it was going to be harder to keep her safe. Thank goodness, the waitress hadn't said anything about time gates.

Silas relaxed as their conversation turned to the

Abbey and the Arthurian legends. After a few minutes he sat back and shook his head. 'You put me to shame, you know. You know more about the history of this place, and you're an Aussie.'

Beth leaned forward and her fragrance surrounded him. 'My interest started when I came over here in my teens. My first degree major was British Constitutional History. Your country fascinates me.'

'I guess that's why you're so interested in the diaries.'

'Partly, but also because Alice's life fascinates me. Apparently she was a feisty woman who knew what she wanted, and wouldn't listen to the family. Mum said she didn't suffer fools gladly. But reading what she left behind gives me a whole different view of who she was, and what she felt. I wish I'd got to meet her.'

Silas literally had to bite his tongue. He wanted to tell Beth that Alice had been a lovely woman, and how much she was actually like her. When he'd met her at the festival, she'd had thick grey braids and she'd mentioned that she had been auburn in her youth.

'Do you think it would be all right if I read some of the journals too? Maybe I can get a sense of her too.'

A wide smile creased Beth's cheeks. 'Oh, that would be fabulous. You might be able to help me pin a time on some of her travels.

He raised an eyebrow. 'You never know, I might.'

True to his word, Silas apologised to the waitress when he paid the bill.

She put her hand on his arm. 'Trust your feelings, sir, if you stand on the meeting place. You won't be disappointed.'

'I'm sure I won't be,' he said as he gave her a generous tip, feeling more settled.

Beth was staring across the fields towards Glastonbury Tor. She'd pulled the green head piece over her hair again and tucked her hair beneath it. After she pulled her coat together and buttoned the top two buttons, she slipped her arm through his. 'Come on, we're going for a walk. We can check out the crossing place in the field and stand on it and both feel mellow and happy.'

Any mellowness or happiness that Silas had been feeling disappeared like a shot as he tried to think of a reason to go home via the road, but Beth tugged at his arm.

'I know you too well. Come on, lazybones, we need the exercise and the grass is dry. It hasn't snowed since Monday, and anyway we both have sturdy boots on.'

One last ditch attempt. He pulled her close and nuzzled his lips against her neck. 'I can think of a much better way to exercise than walk across a slushy field full of cows.'

She shook her head.

'And I promise I know lots of ways to make you feel mellow and happy too.' He pulled back and winked at her.

'I know you do.' Beth giggled, but she wouldn't budge. 'You can go back to the cottage if you want, but I'm going that way. She pulled her arm from his, pointed in the direction of the Tor and strode away from him. She looked over her shoulder with a laugh when he followed her along the road, past the village store and the small church. 'Good man! And you know what, I think this way's shorter so we'll get back home even faster.'

It was quicker, Silas knew that. He'd travelled the path from the stones to the pub on many occasions when he and Bear had visited Davy in the cottage over the years. The village looked as quaint as it always had back then. Geese dotted the village green, and the whitewashed walls of the pub contrasted with the washed out blue of the sky. Low bushy trees blocked the view past the pub.

'We have to cross two fields to get to the stones," he said as he caught up to her. 'Are you really sure you want to go cross country?'

'I am.'

A couple of black and white cows stood

silently and watched them as Silas took Beth's hand and crossed to the middle of the first field.

If she was so damn set on going there, he wasn't going to let her out of his sight, or let go of her hand. She chatted happily beside him as they skirted around the cows.

'They're so pretty, but I'm a city girl, so let's not go too close. Where did you grow up, Silas? In the city or the country?' She tipped her head up and smiled at him and a shaft of longing shook him to the core.

'In the Irish countryside. My parents had a dairy farm.'

'Had? Are they still alive?'

He shook his head. 'No.'

'I'm sorry to hear that.' Beth squeezed his fingers. 'Recently?'

'No, a long time ago.'

'Do you have family? Brothers and sisters?'

'No,' he said slowly. 'There's just me, I sold the farm.'

'So where's home for you now?'

'At the moment,' he leaned over and put his arm around her shoulders, 'it's living in Davy's cottage next to a smashing looking redhead.'

'Smashing? I've never been called smashing before. Or with such a lovely Irish accent.'

Silas tugged on her hand as they reached the turnstile where the two fields intersected, until Beth turned to face him. The closer they got to the stones, the more jumpy he was getting. He ran his hands down her arms and then linked them around her back.

'You are beautiful. Is that better?' He lowered his head and she tilted hers up to meet him, until his lips were a breath away from hers. ' I need to tell you how I feel about you, Beth.'

'You already have, and you've shown me.' Her breath warmed his lips as she whispered back to him.

'I need to tell you again now. And I need you to know that you're stuck with me for a very long time. I've been trying to find my home, where I belong, and I have now that I've met you.'

'That's good, because you're stuck with me too. I don't want you to go anywhere either.'

Her mouth was soft beneath his. He coaxed gently and her lips opened to welcome him. Warmth eased the tension that had been holding him in its grip the closer they'd got to the stones. Beth's hands crept around his neck and she pushed against him. Her perfume, the soft rose fragrance reminded him of spring, and he could see the honeysuckle and the roses that would hang on the trellis between the two cottages, and hear the lazy hum of the bees.

Beth tensed in his arms and moved her lips from his, and emptiness grabbed at him like a claw. 'Listen. What's that humming sound?'

'Just the wind?' he offered lamely. 'Come on, let's go home. I think it's going to rain.'

She looked at him as though he was mad. 'There's not a cloud in the sky. 'Look, there's the stones. Come and feel mellow and then we'll go back to the cottage.' Her laugh hung in the air around him as she ran ahead towards the three grey stones that were covered with sunlight.

Silas ran after her and glanced down at his watch, and his world stopped.

'No, Beth. Stop. Wait for me, Don't go any closer.'

But she kept running towards them, her emerald green coat flapping behind her, unable to hear him over the humming as it reached its crescendo.

Silas felt as though he was running under water; it was like the dream when he was taking steps and not getting anywhere.

'Stop!' he yelled again, desperately looking at his watch. It was a minute before noon.

If only he'd thought to check the time when they'd left the pub, he could have taken her on a detour. 'No!'

Beth reached the large marker on the end and turned to wave. His world stopped as she smiled at him. All Silas could see was her emerald green coat contrasting with the grey of the stone as she reached out to touch it at shoulder level on the edge.

Her eyes held his as the flash of blue light arced into the sky and she was gone.

Chapter 19

Beth's legs were cold and her coat was wet. She opened her eyes and blinked, wondering why her bed was so cold. She looked down confused; the light was fading and she was outside.

Sitting on the damp grass in the middle of a field at dusk.

A frown stretched her forehead, and she put a shaking hand to her head; it was aching and her eyes were gritty. There was a large rock behind her, and she leaned on it trying to remember what had happened.

Silas? Where is he?

They'd had breakfast and then they'd walked over to the marker stone in the field. She'd waved to him and he had screamed "no" as he'd run towards her, a look of horror stretching his features into a grimace.

Maybe someone attacked me?

Beth pulled herself to her feet and closed her eyes as her head spun. She leaned her head against the stones, but her legs crumpled beneath her and she couldn't stop herself sliding to the ground.

When she opened her eyes again, darkness had fallen, and a few lonely stars pricked the black velvet of the sky above.

It was bitterly cold. She shivered and tried to stop her teeth chattering as she pulled herself to her feet. After a moment, the spinning stopped, but the nausea remained and she swallowed.

What if they'd hurt Silas? He *must* be hurt because he wouldn't have left her out here by herself. Beth stood there, looking around trying to remember which way to go. Fear gripped her insides and she gagged as she fought the bile rising in her throat.

Her phone. It was in her coat pocket and she could use the flashlight and the compass to find her way back to the village and call the police.

She dug into her pocket and pulled it out, and pressed the home button. The backlight came on, but there were no apps on the screen. Fear rippled through her again, as something scurried along the ground behind the rocks and she backed away. There was something wrong with her phone; it must have broken as she fell.

The sound came from her left and she raised her head, suddenly alert. It came again, a snatch of a whisper and footsteps coming across the grass towards her. She shoved her phone back into her pocket and pressed herself against the stone. Closing her eyes, she held her breath listening to the voices.

'They sent a party out to repair the crossing, because the bridge was burned. There was a skirmish and Lord Branton was injured.' The voices got closer, and Beth pressed herself against the flat stone, willing them to pass along the back of it.

'Is he back from Blackheath then?

'Aye, that he is.' The voices faded as the two men moved into the distance, and she held back the sigh of relief.

'Perhaps that will teach him; he might stay and look after the estate now.'

'That would be excellent.'

Beth leaned forward peering int the darkness, her ears attuned for any sound.

All was quiet.

She stepped forward and screamed as rough hands grabbed her around the waist.

***

After marking the stone with a small rock Silas ran all the way back to the cottage. His breath was ragged and his chest was aching by the time he reached the road and pushed open the gate. He cursed Davy for building that huge wall at the back of the cottages.

A lot of good it had done; it had added a mile to his run to the cottages.

He pushed the door to Beth's cottage so hard it bounced back of the wall and the antique cuckoo clock fell to the floor, squawking and protesting it lay there on its back.

His thoughts were whirling around his head. How the hell had he let Beth get ahead of him and let her reach the stones first? Why hadn't he checked the time?

Because your feelings blinded you to common sense, a little voice nagged at him.

Love struck, that's what I was.

Twenty-four hours had to pass before he could follow her at noon tomorrow; he had to talk to Davy, but he was reluctant to call him. Silas stood with one hand on the door and the other holding his head; how the hell was he going to wait so long to follow Beth?

He could try following her at midnight, but the chances of getting an accurate time gate would be risky. He couldn't chance it; he could end up hundreds of years away from her.

One simple job had been given to him and he'd blown it in less than a week.

But he had to call Davy. Silas had only ever travelled the same path, and he had to be sure he followed Beth to the right time. Davy knew so much more about the travel and the time gates than Silas did. They'd only travelled back and forth from their time, 1971, but Alice had told Davy about all the other times she'd visited.

It had to be in her journals; he knew Beth hadn't read about it yet, or she would have mentioned it to him. She was still unsure if she was reading fiction or a personal diary. Silas had felt guilty each time she'd wondered aloud what they were over the past week, because he knew that the journals were a chronicle of Alice's life.

He walked to the kitchen and reached for a glass and filled it with cold water, staring through the window to the fields as he drank. Somewhere, some time, Beth was out there.

Chapter 20

'You fucking what?' David's voice was like cold steel as he flung the blanket back and strode to the window.

Megan sat up in the bed and pushed her hair back from her eyes as she tried to wake up. David's phone had trilled just before dawn, waking them both from a deep sleep.

She climbed out of bed and padded barefoot across the room. Dawn wasn't far off and the ocean shimmered with a silver hue. The fronds of the palm tree outside the large window hung motionless in the still of the early morning, but the tension in the air was thick.

'Oh, fuck, Silas. How the hell did that happen?'

Megan tugged at her husband's arm and mouthed her concern as he listened. 'What's wrong?'

David put one arm around her, holding her close and shook his head. She waited as he listened to the voice at the other end of the phone.

Silas.

It had to be Beth. Something had happened to Beth. Megan put her hand to her stomach as it turned; it was bad enough most mornings when she got out of bed, but this time, fear ran its icy fingers down her throat and she knew she was going to vomit.

Because she knew what must have happened.

Oh God. Megan could remember how scared she was when it happened to her, but luckily David had been there when she'd arrived.

And Silas. And Bear.

She put her hand over her mouth and made a dash for the luxury ensuite.

She'd been in the bathroom for a few minutes before David pushed open the door. The worst of the sickness had passed, and now she was resting, weak and tired..

'Are you okay, sweetheart?' He picked up a flannel and ran it under the cold tap before coming over to where she was sitting on the tiled bench at the edge of the huge spa bath.

She took the flannel and wiped her face. 'I'm fine. What's happened? Is it Beth?'

David sat on the bench beside her and nodded.

'Yes. Slim couldn't stop her.'

'She knew what she was doing?'

'No, it was a stupid accident. She insisted on seeing the stones because someone at the pub told her about the ley lines, and she ran ahead of Slim. She reached the stone before he did, and it was right on noon. She went straight away.'

Megan held David's gaze? 'Where to?' she whispered.

David shrugged. 'Slim doesn't know, but he marked the spot on the stone where she had her hand.

Megan frowned and her stomach gurgled again. 'What does that have to do with it.'

'The position of your hand determines your time destination. Alice told me that. We always how and where—Slim and I still do—to pinpoint our time.'

Megan's stomach clenched. Davy had given up his time for her and said he was never going back. 'Should we go back to Glastonbury and help him?'

David shook his head. 'No, Slim is going tomorrow. Midday their time.'

'But what if Beth arrived somewhere that isn't safe and how will he find her?'

'We have to stay positive and have faith, love. I found you.'

'But Slim and Beth have no connection! He was just supposed to be keeping her safe.'

'They do. The same thing has happened to them, that we experienced. Slim is distraught.'

'What do you mean?'

'He loves her, Megan, and if anything will help him find her, that will be the key.

Chapter 21

Beth widened her eyes as the man tugged at her coat.

'Come on, you. We're taking you back to the manor house.'

All she could think of was that the man had mentioned Branton before.

Was it the same Branton from Alice's journal? Was he still living around here?

Their accents were rough and the dialect was one that she was unfamiliar with. She shook her head and tried to pull away.

'I'm fine, thank you. I'll find my way home.'

The man dropped his hand briefly and there was enough starlight for Beth to see him turn to his friend.

'God's truth. It's a lass.'

The other man reached out and took her arm in a firm grip. 'Aye, but did you hear her words? They have a touch of Cornish in them. We can't be too careful.'

'I'm not Cornish. I'm Australian.'

The grip on her arm tightened. 'If you're from the continent, all the more reason for you to be watched.'

'*Australia*, not Austria.' Frustration filled Beth and she tried to pull away. 'Please. I just need to go back to my cottage. It's just over there,' —she gestured in the direction of the high fence that separated the two cottages from the field—'and I'll be fine to go back alone.'

The other man took her other arm, and before she knew what was happening, they were leading—half dragging—her back across the fields in the direction of the village. Her dizziness had passed, and her strength was returning. As the blood pumped back through her limbs, the numbing cold eased. But fear stayed with her.

Who were these men? What had happened to her and where was Silas?

She questioned them as they hurried her along, but they ignored her. Soon, lights appeared ahead, and Beth let out a sigh of relief. The pub would surely be open, and she could use the phone there to call the police and express her concern about Silas and tell them what had happened to her.

Not that she really knew what had actually happened. Her head was fuzzy and if she turned too quickly, it still left her dizzy. They turned to the left and the road was uneven beneath her feet and she stumbled.

A drystone wall edged the field and Beth frowned. This wasn't the way to the village. She tried to stop, but the two men tugged her along.

'Where are you taking me.' Despite trying to stay calm, she couldn't keep the fear from her voice.

'To the manor house.'

'Where is that? I don't know it.'

The laugh that came from the man on her left frightened Beth; it held menace.

She made a small sound and the other man laughed. 'Starting to get worried, are ye? The duke's nae here to save you. We know where he is. He's getting closer but he won't be saving you.'

'I have no idea what you're talking about, and I insist that you let me go immediately.'

The only response was a tighter grip, and faster pace. Beth was suddenly conscious of the cold again; damp had seeped into her boots until she could barely feel her feet.

'Lord Branton will decide what your future is.' The taller man pointed ahead. 'The stables are lit; he must be back.'

'Good. We can be done with this woman.'

A large building loomed in front of them, soft yellow light dancing in the lead lighted windows. Another man stood in a small building at the end of the path and he stepped out and challenged them.

'It's us, Peterkin and Thomas. We found a spy lurking along the road.'

'I wasn't on the road,' Beth protested. 'And I'm not a spy.' This situation was surreal, and she wondered if she'd stumbled onto the set of a television program. Now that there was light from the torch the man in front of them held high, she could see that they were dressed in costume, and a measure of relief filled her. The two men let her go and she put a hand against her chest.

'Thank God. It is a set. You must have been expecting someone else. Look, I don't know how I got there. All I can remember is that I woke up near the stones. I must have fainted or something and my partner must have gone for help.'

'Partner? There are more of you? How many?' The man's voice was full of urgency; he turned and looked back the way they'd come.

'Yes, my partner. He won't be far away,' she explained patiently. 'We live over in the cottages.

There was a commotion at the entrance behind the man at the door, and the double wooden doors opened.

'What is going on down here?' A tall man—in costume like the others—strode over to them. His hair was as black as a crow's and his cheekbones were high and angular. His voice was full of anger and Beth took a step back.

'We found a Cornishwoman hiding near the road. We think she is spying for the Pretender.'

'Oh, for God's sake, where are the cameras?' Beth exclaimed. 'Enough of this carry on. Just let me call my partner, and I'll be away from you and you can get on with whatever it is you're doing.'

'Lord Branton, where shall we put her?'

Lord Branton? Beth's mouth dropped open as she stared at the man they had addressed.

He came closer and as he stared down at her the blood drained from his face.

'Alice? By the gods, Alice! You came back?'

He turned to the men. 'Be gone. Leave us alone.'

Chapter 22

Beth's cheek was pressed against rough, wet wool and she stiffened as the man called Branton held her close. He kept his face against her headpiece and didn't speak for a long time, but his body trembled against hers. The smell of damp wool and perspiration was cloying, but she stayed pressed against him; her fear had receded and she sensed this man would not do her harm. Sympathy for him overtook her fear. The other two men had frightened her, and now she was calmer she tried to think.

'I have missed you so much.' His fingers gripped her waist, but the hold was gentle. 'I thought I had lost you. Oh, Alice—' His voice broke and Beth swallowed.

Slowly she moved back out of his hold, unsure of what to say. Her mind was spinning; who was this man who had mistaken her for Alice? Where was she? It had to be the Branton in Alice's diary, but the setting didn't make sense.

Alice had loved her Branton, that had

come through clearly in her words, but she had left him.

Why?

As Beth stepped back, she looked around the room that he had led her to; the men who had dragged her here had disappeared instantly on his command. They were in the middle of a large room; the walls were richly panelled with timber and the long narrow windows with lead lighted glass with coloured images filling each space. The few pieces of furniture were made of timber, and were austere.

Beth looked up and put her hand to her head as blue eyes like Silas's held hers, full of emotion. His mouth worked, but no words came out. As she stepped back he held out one hand to her. His fingers were long, and clean. On the middle finger of his right hand, he wore a large gold ring with some sort of crest engraved into it.

'Where am I?' she asked softly.

He looked at her closely. 'Your voice is different, and the lilt of your words has changed, Alice.'

Beth wasn't sure how to respond. If she denied being Alice, she could be returned to those men. The realisation that she had stumbled into something unknown ran though her thoughts, and fear and uncertainty took hold.

But it was best to be truthful. IF she was caught out in a lie, he may not help her.

'No. I am not Alice, I am her niece. I have heard that I do resemble her.'

His voice changed. 'Why do you lie, my sweet? What are you afraid of. Alice?'—the pleading in his voice almost brought her to tears—'you know I would never hurt you.'

'I am not Alice. I do not know you. I am her *niece*.'

His eyes clouded as she watched. 'But Alice was alone; she had no family.' His brows lowered. 'Or that was the truth I was told.'

'When?' Beth asked. 'When did Alice tell you that? When did she visit you?

'|You left me in autumn, but you— she—' his expression was perplexed—'went before the harvest was finished. You left my bed in the dark of night, Alice. Why?'

Beth swallowed and her hands were trembling. 'When was this, which wheat harvest? How long ago?'

His brow creased in a frown. 'Last autumn. A full year ago.'

'But when? Beth insisted. 'What year was it?' An awful feeling was creeping though her bones as she looked around, and the fear returned. Not of this man, but of the situation she was in.

'Last September in the year of our Lord, 1496.'

##

Beth blinked and pushed away the hand that was holding a foul smelling concoction on front of her nose. She was sitting by a window with a soft cushion beneath her. As her senses returned, she realised she was sitting in a window seat and the man called Branton was seated at the other end. An unfamiliar woman was trying to hold a small bottle beneath her nose.

Beth coughed and shook her head. The smell was indescribable. 'I'm fine. Thank you.'

Branton waved his hand and the woman bobbed a curtsey and scurried off, closing the door behind her. This room was smaller than the one they had been in before she had fainted.

Again. Twice in one day.

A cold feeling crept back up into her chest and for a moment she thought she was going to pass out again as she recalled what he had said. She fought it and swallowed.

1496.

In a flash it all came together for Beth. Alice's journals, the talk of Jules in the village shop about travelling.

'Are you feeling better now?' His voice

was wary and Beth looked across at Branton.

Lord Branton.

The love of Great Aunt Alice's life. He was a fine-looking man, but it was the concern on his face that convinced Beth that she could trust him.

Perhaps not with the truth, but with keeping her safe until she figured out how she could get back to Silas.

He knew.

Silas knew.

Silas had done as much as he could to keep her away from the stones. The look of horror on his face when she had touched the warm stone was all she needed to remember.

Snippets of conversation between David and Silas, and Megan and David came back to her.

They all knew.

The high fence at the back of the cottages, and everyone trying to tell her that she shouldn't stay at the cottage.

Why don't we go away on a trip? Leave the cottages. Get to know each other. There must be other places you'd like to see? I could take you to Ireland.

Her mother's insistence that Great Aunt Alice had been unwell, and her determination that Beth leave the diaries alone.

Why do you want to know all that? I know enough to tell you that things need to be left alone.

Leave. Them. Alone.

I would be so much happier if you left the cottage.. It's not a good place to be.

They all knew. The stones were a portal to the past. Alice's travels had been a chronicle of that.

'Are you with me? Your thoughts seem a hundred miles away.'

Beth looked across at Branton. 'What shall I call you?'

In the soft light from the lamp burning on a small table n front of the window seat, it was hard to see his expression. 'Branton is my name. And yours?'

'Beth,' she replied.

'Elisabeth?'

'No, just Beth. And I am well, thank you. I have received a couple of shocks today, and it is not like me to faint.'

'You are not Alice. I knew that when I carried you into the parlour.' His voice was filled with sadness and the despair tore at Beth's heart. 'Do you know where she is? Is she well? Is she happy?'

Beth smoothed her fingers over the soft wool of her coat. She took a breath and lifted her head and held his gaze. His eyes were sad, and his mouth was set in a straight line as though he knew what she was about to say.

'Alice has passed on.'

The cry of grief that tore from his throat brought tears to Beth's eyes. Her throat ached so much that she had to swallow before she could speak. She moved along the window seat and took his hand. 'I can tell you that she loved you, and that it broke her heart to leave you. She told me,'—Beth knew it wasn't a lie because the diaries were a window to Alice's truth—'how much she loved you and how hard it was to leave.'

And no matter where I am, I will never forget these months. The thought of leaving him is breaking my heart, but I have to go. I can't stay with him.

It all made sense to Beth now, Alice's constant mention of where and when, and her words, time is fleeting. Seize each opportunity. Make the most of every minute.

'In that why you came? To tell me she has gone?'

'In a way, perhaps it was,' Beth said slowly.

'Thank you.' He lifted his head and his voice was strained. 'Let us not speak of it again. I am sorry for the way that my men treated you. But why were you on the road so late in the night? It is not a safe time for anyone to be travelling,'

Beth shook her head, and then smothered a yawn 'It's a long story. I have travelled a long way today.'

'I am sorry. I have been most unwelcoming. I will call my housekeeper and she will take you to a guest room upstairs.'

'Thank you. I would appreciate that.' Beth went to stand as he did, but he gestured for her to remain where she was. 'Would you tell me one thing before you leave me?'

He paused and nodded. 'If I can.'

'Tell me why it is not safe? What is happening. Is it a war? Is there a battle?'

Beth was torn; now she knew that Alice had decided to come back and be with her love, but should she tell him, that she came back and he wasn't here.

Much soul searching, and two years of planning and putting my affairs in order, and now I was here again.. I had no fear that he would not be waiting for me. He had promised he would wait if I changed my mind, given me his heart and I knew he would be happy that I had returned. The light was dying and he would be in from the fields.

This time I would stay, and make my life

with him. It had taken many, many months to come to that decision, but the love I held for him in my heart was too strong to ignore. I knew it was a lifetime but—

She had arrived in the midst of a battle and when she had come to the manor, Branton had been gone. It was sort of making sense. Beth frowned.

Was it before this time?

Or was it in the future? Trying to figure out, how the crossing of time worked was beyond her. Maybe Alice had tried and come back again in the future?

Maybe she shouldn't have told Branton that she was dead.

'There is no war yet, but there may be.'

'Can you tell me about it?'

Branton sat beside her. 'It's a long story. Perhaps one for in the new day?'

'Now please. It will help me to understand why I need to keep a look out. I will rest better if I know.'

'Wait here.' He rose and went to the door and rang a bell.'

The housekeeper must have been hovering outside the door as she appeared straight away.

'Would you please bring us some refreshments, and prepare a room for our guest,' Branton asked.

They sat quietly and it wasn't long before the housekeeper had brought a tray of food and placed it on the table beside the lamp.. Beth looked with interest at the food: dried figs and almonds on a wooden tray, and what looked like cider in a metal tankard.

Branton offered her the tray and she lifted a tankard and sipped. It was more bitter than the cider she was used to.

'There is a man who claimed his entitlement to the throne seven years ago. He has claimed that he is Richard of Shrewsbury and that when he and his brother, Edward were locked in the tower by their uncle Richard, he was eventually freed and only his brother was murdered.'

'The princes in the tower,' Beth murmured.

'Yes, they were imprisoned when they were but nine and twelve.'

'Supposedly in preparation for Edward's forthcoming coronation as king. But, Richard took the throne for himself and the boys disappeared.'

'Yes. You are a well-informed young woman, Mistress Beth.'

She nodded demurely, wondering if a young woman of that time would be au fait with history.

'He claimed he had been spared by the murderers because of his age and innocent, but was sworn to secrecy under oath that he would not reveal his true identity for a number of years. Richard says he has been on the continent under the protection of Yorkist loyalists. His guardian returned to England and Richard—or the supposed Richard—landed in Kent and declared his identity.

'So why is it now unsafe here? I hear there has been a battle?'

Branton lifted the tankard and took a drink. Beth was pleased to see that he seemed less upset since he had been talking to her. She was still having trouble believing that she was in the fifteenth century listening to a firsthand account of history as it unfolded.

'Many believe that is claim is true and just. Some perhaps as they see it as an opportunity to overthrow Henry. He poses a significant threat and the kind has declared him an imposter.'

'I have heard that several years ago he had much support.' She couldn't help herself. 'Simon de Montfort and Sir William Stanley supported his claims.'

'That they did. But you are aware of their fate?'

Beth nodded. 'Yes, they were beheaded at

the Tower. Surely it is a long way from here.'
Beth sat up straight and that creeping fear
returned. She had assumed that she was in
Glastonbury where she had left through the
stones. Maybe she was somewhere else. Her
heart raced, but Branton's next words reassured
her.

'No, they reached Exeter. His Cornish
army is advancing on Taunton, only twenty
miles from here.' He sat rigid and his hand
clenched in front of him. Two thousand
Cornishmen died at the Battle of Blackheath in
June. I do not want to see innocent men die
again'

'You were there?'

He nodded. 'When Alice left me, I lost
interest in the farm.'

'But you are back now?

'Yes. Seeing the futility of that battle made
me realise that my place is here, looking after
my tenants, and my farm workers. I don't want
to see that happen again, so it is imperative that
you stay here until the danger is over.'

'But—'

He held up his hand. 'We will speak more
tomorrow. I will get Mistress Oatley to take
you up now. Please be assured you are safe
while ever you are in my house.'

Beth stood and he grasped her hands. 'You

have given me sad news today, but I have closure and I thank you for that.'

Chapter 23

Silas prepared himself as best he could. He changed into a pair of beige loose trousers, and a white shirt, before pulling on a pair of sturdy walking boots. A long black coat and a soft woollen hat completed an outfit that would not look out of place in many times. The problem was, he had no idea where Beth had ended up, and how he could fit in until he found her. He'd had no sleep, and the morning had dragged by.

Finally, it was almost eleven o'clock and he stuffed some apples and bread into a plain cotton bag that he'd found on a hook in the laundry room. Two of Beth's T-shirts had been sitting on the washing machine, and when he picked them up and inhaled her perfume, helpless desolation had washed over him.

Silas pulled himself together quickly. He was Beth's only chance of her getting back. Calm and considered thinking and planning was essential or he would have little chance of finding her. He slung the bag over his shoulder, pulled his coat on and opened the front door. The weather had cleared and the sky was bright for early January. The fields were deserted, and not even the cows came over to see what he was doing as he hurried across to the markers. He reached the three stones and looked around. Even though it was a bright day, the sun was low in the winter sky, making a longer shadow than he would have liked.

But it had been the same yesterday when Beth had gone through the gate so he just had to have faith that all would be the same. Davy had always maintained that it was his love for Megan that had helped them find each other across time, so Silas focused his thoughts on Beth as he waited for midday to approach. The minutes ticked away slowly.

Her glorious red hair rippling though his fingers, her translucent skin, her beautiful eyes holding his as he made love to her. The silkiness of her skin beneath his fingers; her rose perfume . . .

Silas swallowed as he looked at the mark where he had scratched the stone yesterday. The low humming began and he waited until the alarm on his phone dinged; he had set it so that he placed his hands on the stone at the stroke of noon

The ping sounded and his placed his palm flat on the mark on the stone and closed his eyes. Fear was the last thing on his mind as he spun in the vortex.

Beth's beautiful face filled his vision and he focused his attention on that as he followed her.

The road was muddy and crowded with many people making their way to the town ahead. Silas put his head down, and pulled his coat around him. He listened to the voices around him trying to pinpoint the time he was in. The clothing of the men around him consisted mainly of tunics over short woollen trousers and sturdy boots. Despite the cold, few wore coats, and the smell of unwashed bodies pervaded the cold air.

It sure as hell wasn't 1971.

He listened to the nuances of the dialect, and when he had worked it out, he caught up to the two men in front of him. They appeared to be a father and son, carrying a basket full of turnips, and a small cage with three scrawny chickens in it.

'Aye, good morn,' he said as he caught up to them. 'Can you tell me how far to the market?'

'Another two miles to Glastonbury, if that's where ye are heading. We were off to Taunton, another twenty miles farther but we changed our minds when the news came through to our village yesterday.' He lowered his voice and looked around furtively and must have decided that Silas wasn't a threat. 'Depends if ye are selling or buying?'

'Buying,' Silas said, but didn't elaborate.

'Well, Glastonbury is the best market if ye are after wool. And safer than Taunton.'

Silas nodded his thanks and went to pass them, but the man stayed him with one hand. 'But take care. There is trouble afoot, so keep your wits about you.'

'Trouble?' Silas concentrated on keeping the Irish from his voice.

'The Cornishmen are on their way to Taunton, so we've heard. Six thousand of them in Exeter and the king is heading to Glastonbury. Dangerous times.'

'The king?' Silas widened his eyes. 'Why would the king come to Glastonbury?' he asked, cursing himself for his lack of knowledge of English history.

'Henry has sent Lord Daubeney to deal with the rebels.'

Henry? Silas thought. That narrowed it down to eight possible kings, but he knew it put him back at least to the sixteenth century.

'Rebels? I've not heard of this.'

'Where have ye been, man?'

'I've been working at my uncle's farm and he is a dour man, who does not welcome visitors. He has sent me to the market to look for—'

Shit, what would he be looking for in a medieval market?

'More sheep? You will be better at Glastonbury. Where is your farm?'

'Pilton.'

'Glastonbury will suit you. It is not far to move your stock.'

'Thank ye. I am grateful. Tell me more about these rebels.' He settled beside the man and kept his pace in time with his.

'Well, they say it is Richard the Fourth who has come ashore at Lands End.'

'Richard the Fourth?' Silas screwed his face up in an exaggerated frown. Even with his basic secondary school history he knew there had only been three King Richards.

'Aye, he has gathered supporters from Cornwall and they declared him Richard the Fourth on Bodmin Moor this past month.'

Silas nodded, unsure of what to say.

'But take care, man. There is trouble afoot. Trust no one, man or woman. Tho' you should be safe in Glastonbury.'

Silas nodded and wen to doff his hat as the pair moved on ahead. 'Ah, just one question,' he called.

'Aye?' The man seemed anxious to get

ahead.

'Have you been on the road long? My sister was with me and we became separated. Her cloak is green.'

The man looked at Silas strangely, and then shook his head. 'I've seen no woman in a green cloak.'

This time Silas touched his hand to his hat and nodded his thanks. He put his head down and trudged along the road towards the town.

Where would Beth have gone? Would she have sought shelter once she realised what had happened? Or would she have realised what had happened? It sounded as though they—if Beth was indeed here and he prayed that she was—had arrived in the middle of a dangerous political situation.

When he had arrived, he'd spent time at the stones looking for any sign that she'd been there, but there had been nothing. The landscape was different, and a road made its way close to the marker stones.

He would start looking in the town; he had more chance of someone having seen her there. A woman with red hair in a green cloak would surely make an impression.

If he couldn't find her, he had no idea what he would do. An icy chill of helplessness wormed its way through his gut.

As he made his way to the market town, Silas willed himself to stay strong.

Chapter 24

The market at Glastonbury was crowded and busy. Silas was taller than most of the people who thronged around him, and he scoured the crowd for the sight of an emerald green cloak.

But there was nothing. No sign of Beth.

He wandered past the various stalls, looking from left to right, desperately hoping to catch sight of her. The market was busy, but he only gave a fleeting glance to the various stalls: food stalls that made his mouth water and bolts of cloth of all colours spilling over the front of the stalls, chickens squawking in cages, and a confused rooster crowing at the end of the row. A plethora of stalls that went for at least a quarter of a mile ahead. The hawkers, carrying their wares in baskets and calling to the crowd milling between the stalls were no different to those at Camden Market in London in the twenty-first century.

Silas knew that market towns were often near castles and monasteries. The abbey at Glastonbury was famous, and he had visited it a number of times in the past—or in the future—

but to his surprise, this market was located along the edge of a wide canal that appeared to continue to the river. There had been no canal in Glastonbury when he had visited it, either in 1971 or in Beth's time.

Heraldic flags flew at regular intervals and the smell of roasting meat made his stomach gurgle. He hadn't eaten for twenty-four hours and food had been the last thing on his mind after Beth had disappeared and he'd had to wait a full day to follow her. The brunch they had shared at the pub at Pilton seemed to be aeons ago; Silas shrugged and shook his head as a sense of disbelief engulfed him.

And it was.

Aeons ago.

If his estimations were correct, he'd gone back to the fourteenth or fifteenth century. The abbey was still intact; he'd passed the buildings on the way in to the market as the crowd had pushed him along.

He knew the King Henry that the man on the road had spoken of, had to be before Henry the Eighth, and before the time of the dissolution of the monasteries across the country,

For the first time, Silas had an appreciation of Beth's fascination with history. There was so much he didn't know.

He walked along the stalls, looking and watching for a flash of green. Finally hunger got the better of him; if he was to find Beth he had to keep his strength up. He went behind a stall to the edge of the canal, and pulled out the bread he'd packed; it was dry and hard but it was sustenance.

'Blessed St Mary!' The shrill voice caught his attention. 'Why are you sitting here gnawing on a dry hunk of bread when there is tasty food on offer?'

Silas looked up. A matronly woman was bearing down on him flapping her arms like the chickens in the cage he had passed at the last stall.

'I have no spare coin, ma'am.'

Shit, was that the correct form of address?

'I am here to buy sheep, not to sample the wares of the market.' Despite his worry for Beth, Silas stifled a grin. He felt like Simple Simon of the nursery rhyme.'

'I need a brawny man to help me at my stall. My useless husband has gone to the inn. If you help me, sir, I'll see you are fed.'

Silas nodded and after stuffing his bread back into the bag he followed the woman back to the market. She pointed to the bolts of cloth that were in a cart at the bag of her tent-like stall.

'If ye can lift them out and put them on the table, I'll make sure you get a decent meal,' she said.

Silas nodded. 'I am pleased to be of service.' It gave him a valid reason to be here, and would help him blend in with the crowd.

'What's your name, lad?' the woman asked as she pointed to the cart.

'Silas,' he said as he walked over to the cart behind her.

'From the forest?' She opened the timber flap at the back of the wooden cart.

'Aye,' he said. It was getting easier to pick up the dialect the more he spoke, and he hoped that Beth's accent wasn't causing her any trouble. The shaft of worry that hit him thinking of what could happen to her lodged in his chest and his voice was gruff. 'From the forest.' He gestured vaguely to the west.

She looked at him quizzically as he lifted the first bolt of silk and carried it to the stall. 'No, your name means from the forest.

'I didn't know that.'

It didn't take Silas long to unload the cart, and the woman dug into the folds of her cloak and pulled out a silver penny.

'That will feed you.' She handed it to Silas and he nodded his thanks.

'Thank you . . . what is your name?'

'Mistress Clifford.'

'Then thank you, Mistress Clifford. Do you live around here?' he asked.

'No, we came from Exeter, but will not return until the Cornish have been dealt with. My husband said he was seeking accommodation at the inn, but it was an excuse not to unload the cart.'

'If I am still here, I will help you later in the day to pack up.'

'You are a good man.' She pointed to the fields across the canal. 'Dirk Boult sells sheep over there, but don't let him take all your money. He is a charlatan.'

'Mistress Clifford?'

She nodded.

'I am also here to find my . . . sister. She has run away and I am concerned for her welfare. If you see a very pretty young woman with red hair in an dark green cloak, would you tell her that Silas is here looking for her?'

'That I can do. Now off to buy your sheep, lad, and let me get to selling my cloth.'

Chapter 25

A tap on the door roused Beth the next morning. She sat up in the unfamiliar bed, her hair in a messy tangle around her face. She blinked and put a hand to her aching head wondering where on earth she was. She was wearing her underwear, not her PJs. The bed had four timber posts and the walls of the room were panelled in timber squares that replicated the shape of the mullioned windows. On the opposite wall a huge tapestry, richly patterned in blues and golds hung from the ceiling.

'Just a moment,' she called.

The day before came back in a rush when the door opened and Mistress Oatley, the housekeeper in Branton's manor, bustled in with a tray in her hands.

'Good morning, miss. I trust you slept well?' The woman put the tray on the high table beside the bed, crossed to the windows and opened the curtains. Dust motes danced in the pale sunlight that streamed in through the mullioned window.

'I did. Thank you.' Beth sat up and leaned back against the embroidered cover on the feather pillow. The bed had been soft, and she'd slept deep and dreamlessly. Although she had hoped that yesterday's events had been a dream, the presence of the housekeeper, and the strange room, told her it was real, and she was still in an unfamiliar place and time. Beth had no understanding of the circumstances of how she had reached this place—this time—and when she thought about how it seemed that everyone else knew it was possible, anger had built. Alice had known and explored this time. And perhaps other times?

Silas, Megan, David—who else knew about this time travel stuff? Her anger and confusion made it impossible to think rationally.

However, neither anger nor worry were going to get her out of the predicament she had found herself in, so Beth knew she had to face the day and try to find her way back. It had to be easy if they had all done it before her. She swallowed and fought back the heavy feeling that had settled in her chest.

The housekeeper lifted a small china teapot and poured tea into a delicate cup with a gold rim. Beth picked up the cup; it reminded her of some of the pieces they had found in the trunks at Aunt Alice's house after she'd passed on. All of the old things that they had found there and dismissed as op shop rubbish now had a different possible source: the old-fashioned shoes, the china, even the leather-bound journals. Had Alice brought them back with her from her travels?

'His lordship suggested that perhaps you might like to come to the market with me when you rise,' the housekeeper said as she picked up Beth's coat and folded it. Her eyes widened as she looked at the sewing of it, and the brand tag that sat beneath the wide collar.

'That would be interesting, thank you,' Beth said. With some luck she could get her bearings and figure out where she was in relation to the stones. If Alice could travel back and forth, so could she. Uncertainty warred with determination as she vowed to get back home. All she had done was touched the largest stone and that had brought her here. So theoretically, all she had to do was find the field with the stones, touch the big one and go home.

'He has been called out to deal with an estate matter but Lord Branton asked me to tell you that he will meet with you later in the day.'

Beth nodded, but was quietly hoping that she would be gone by then.

Heat ran up her neck as the housekeeper bent down and removed the chamber pot from beneath the bed. It had taken Beth a good ten minutes last night to realise there was no bathroom, and to find the china pot.

'I will bring you some hot water, and when you come down, we shall leave. If that suits you mistress?'

Beth nodded. 'I won't be long.'

When Mistress Oatley closed the door quietly, Beth put the teacup aside carefully, climbed down from the high bed and hurried across to the window. She put one hand on the glass and leaned down slightly so she could see between the lead lighted seams in the glass.

Green fields dotted with sheep stretched as far as she could see. Relief flooded through her as she spotted the familiar sight of Glastonbury Tor. At least she was in the same place. She pushed open the window and the fragrance of the flowers surrounded her.

Below the window was an enclosed courtyard filled with flowers. Beth frowned; one day ago, she had been in the dead of winter, but it appeared that it was summer here, even though she had been cold last night when she'd awoken on the damp grass. A tangle of roses and honeysuckle climbed the brick wall at the back of the courtyard, and delphiniums and hollyhocks filled the garden in a riot of colour. It was just as she imagined the cottage garden would be like in the spring and summer.

A niggle of worry tugged at her. If she had arrived here—
in 1497 if what Branton had told her was the truth—it was a different time of year to when she'd left.

God. Of course, it was. It was six centuries different, so what difference did a change in season make? She gripped the window sill as she stared at the garden, trying to dispel the sick feeling that roiled in her stomach.

What if I can't find the stones? What if I find them and nothing happens when I touch them?

What if she ended up in a different place entirely where the welcome was not as friendly as the one she'd received here?

The door opened, and Beth pulled the window shut as Mistress Oatley carried a jug across to the screened area to the right of the bed. Beth's eyes widened; the jug was covered with large pink flowers and had an ornate handle.

It was the same jug that was on the marble washstand in Great Aunt Alice's cottage.

Alice had been here. And she'd taken something back with her. Confusion whirled in Beth's thoughts and she put her hand to her head. But if Alice took it back when she left, it wouldn't be here.

Unless she had come back again?

Beth recalled the journal entry when she had come back the second time and the manor house had been shut up.

Maybe Alice *had* come back again? Maybe that was when she had taken the jug back.

'Are you feeling poorly, dear?' The housekeeper put the jug down and came across to her as Beth sat on the small footstool at the end of the bed. 'You are very pale.'

'Just a little dizzy,' Beth said seizing the opportunity. 'I haven't been well, and my memory is not as good as it should be. Can you tell me what time of year it is? The flowers are very pretty.'

'Ah, that would Hodges' doing. He is a good gardener.' Mistress Oatley looked at her with a worried frown. 'The garden is in bloom because it is the end of summer. We have just come into August. Did you not know that?'

Beth shook her head. 'No. Ah, yes. I do. I remember now.'

'I shall leave you to finish your tea and wash. I will be going to the market in an hour. If you would prefer to lie abed, that might be better.'

'Oh, no.' Beth stood. 'I am feeling much better now. I want to come with you.'

'Very well. Wait in the parlour when you come down.'

The door closed, and Beth walked over and felt the water in the jug. It was hot, and she picked up the washcloth that the housekeeper had left on the side of the dish. It was made of coarse linen and was a dull grey colour. After washing, she dressed quickly, braided her hair and pulled on the headpiece.

In the light of day, she didn't want to look different and attract unwanted attention.

Mistress Oatley was hovering in the parlour, and nodded briskly when Beth walked in. She held out a large piece of fabric in the same dull grey of the linen cloth. Beth frowned as her fingers brushed the stiff fabric.

'The day is warm. I thought your wool coat may be too hot, so I have a cloak for you to wear today,' the housekeeper said.

'Thank you.' Beth stood still as the woman took her green cloak and put it on the window seat. She then slipped the stiff cloak over Beth's shoulders and then passed her a wicker basket.

'Stay close to me, and don't talk to anyone.'

Beth frowned. Although she had no intention of doing that, it was a strange request. 'Why is that?' she asked.

The woman looked at her long and hard. 'Because of your dialect. We have no need for more questions. It caused enough trouble for the master when the other one disappeared.'

Beth stiffened. 'The other one?'

'The woman who broke the master's heart. It was almost the end of the estate. He went off to fight and—' she waved a dismissive hand— 'if he hadn't returned there was no one left in the family. Who knows what would have become of the farm.'

'Tell me about this other woman. Why do you think I am the same?'

'The way you talk. The way you just appeared. Your clothes with the strange writing on the collars. That is what she wore.' Her lips were set in a straight line. 'At first I thought you were she. You are very much like her.

Beth held the basket tightly. 'I believe the other woman was my aunt, but I have not met her. Can you tell me about her? What was her name?' Her voice was soft, and she held the housekeeper's gaze with hers.

Eventually the woman dropped her eyes first and huffed. 'Her name was Alice. Come on, then. We will miss the best of the goods at the market. I will tell you more about her as we make our way there. But remember—if anyone speaks, put your head down and do not answer.'

Chapter 26

Silas had walked the length of the markets and back again three times. The crowds had increased as residents of outlying villages came to town. As the day passed it became harder to push through the mass of people. The noise and the smell added to the frustration tugging at him, and each time he reached the end of the market stalls with no sign of Beth his worry increased.

His head was aching slightly as it always did after travelling, and his stomach was growling, but Silas was reluctant to spend the silver penny that the kind woman from the stall had given him a couple of hours ago. He'd eaten the food he'd brought with him, and as the day warmed, his thirst was adding to his discomfort. The sun was high in the sky, and noon had passed an hour ago. They'd missed the time gate today and if he found Beth—no, *when*, not if—they would have to wait another twenty-four hours before they could go back to the stones. All he could hope was it was "they", and that Beth was here somewhere, and he would find her soon.

The alternative—or the hundreds and

thousands of them—didn't bear thinking about. Silas wished he'd had more time to talk to Davy about the bloody mechanics of how they'd travelled in the past. He and Bear—most often with Davy—had been so casual about the trip from 1971 to the time that Davy preferred to live in. All that was at stake those times was that they would miss a gig, or miss lunch at the pub.

Now, it was his future at stake, and the safety of the woman he loved.

Silas cursed beneath his breath as he walked past the stalls. He'd elicited strange looks as he'd walked along but had soon discovered the best way to deal with it was to stare them down. He was much taller than the men he encountered and that gave him some advantage.

He turned and headed back towards the township; he would find a stream to drink from and then he'd go back to the stones on the off chance that Beth was there.

'Did you find who you were looking for?' The shrill voice of Mistress Clifford rose above the noise of the crowd and the chickens squawking as he passed her stall.

Silas stopped and shook his head. 'You haven't seen the woman with the green cloak?'

She shook her head. 'If I do see your sister,

would you like me to give her a message?'

'Yes, I am going elsewhere for a while. If you do see her, can you please tell her to wait with you, and I will be back. Her name is Beth. And tell her . . . tell her that Silas is here.'

'Surely she will know you are looking for her already if she has run away?'

Silas thought quickly. 'She does it every time we come to a town, but my sister always comes to her senses. If you tell her I am here, she will wait. I am sure of that.'

Mistress Clifford nodded. 'I will do my best to persuade her. You are a most patient brother.'

'I will be back in an hour.' Now that he had someone else to look out for Beth, and give her a message, he would go back to the stones and then search in the township itself.

'Thank you.' He nodded as he strode away.

As they reached the end of the stone path, Beth turned around and looked back at the fine house. It was a two-storey structure, with a brown shingled roof that peaked at interesting angles. The main house sat amidst rolling green lawns. And the stone path they had walked along to the narrow road was lined with a row of clipped topiary trees on each side. As she leaned forward she could just get a glimpse of a fountain and a small pond at the right of the house. To the left was a small chapel; the coloured glass sparked in the late morning sun.

'How far is it to the market?' Beth asked Mistress Oatley as she followed her through a turnstile into a field dotted with sheep.

'By road it is three miles but cutting across the fields makes it only just over a mile.'

As they walked across the lush green grass Mistress Oatley spoke of Alice and the few months that she spent at the manor.

'You are very like her, Mistress Beth. The same height, the same hair, and very similar in your visage.' Mistress Oatley paused as they reached the top of the hill. 'When she first arrived, I wasn't sure, but when I saw how much the master loved her, I gradually learned what a good person she was. She was willing to help in the kitchens, and in the fields and she was always happy. She did the master a power of good. When she left—' she stared ahead and her voice trailed away—'anyway enough of that now. She has gone, and I suppose you will be soon.'

Beth looked down the hill. A large field spread before them, and her breath stilled as her gaze settled on the three familiar stones in the centre. Strangely she didn't recall a hill when she had run to the stones yesterday, but perhaps the landscape ahead changed over the centuries.

Of course, it would.

'Mistress Oatley?' Beth's voice was low and urgent. 'I need to do something. 'Would you wait here, please? For a moment?' She handed the basket to the housekeeper and took one step towards the field before she turned back. 'I would like to thank you for what you have told me. I have learned much about my aunt.' In the half hour that it had taken them to walk to the market, she felt as though she learned more about her great aunt, than she ever heard from her mother or from reading the journals. 'And for your kindness. I hope that you can also thank Lord Branton for me for his hospitality.'

'Very well.' The words were patient and Beth sensed that the woman understood.

'Thank you, again,' she said.

Hurrying down the hill, Beth kept her eye on the stones. There was no one else in sight. As she reached them, she turned back and waved to the woman waiting at the top of the hill.

As she turned back to the stone marker, she noticed that someone had scratched a mark at her eye level. She stared at it, wondering if it was a name, but as she looked more closely it was just a long yellowish line. Beth walked slowly to the middle stone and took a deep breath. She closed her eyes as she reached out to touch the stone, willing herself to think of home.

But the stone was cold and dead beneath her hands, only the bleating of sheep surrounded her.

She waited and swallowed before she took another deep breath and moved her hands higher.

Chapter 27

Opening her eyes, Beth looked up the hill where Mistress Clifford was waiting patiently. Her breath hitched in a sob as she realised that nothing had happened. She looked down at the grey cloak and the twenty-first century boots that peeked from beneath the folds.

With a sigh she gathered the cloak in her hands and hurried back up the hill. Now that she knew where the stones were, she would come back and keep trying.

She would think about what had happened when she had gone back in time.

Mistress Oatley looked at her quizzically and Beth stopped to catch her breath.

'Thank you. I just wanted to—'

The woman shook her head. 'It is a good place and a bad place and that is all I will say.'

Beth nodded. Taking the wicker basket back, she followed the housekeeper down the hill to a road that led to the east.

Panic was tugging at the edge of her consciousness, and she breathed slowly and evenly to dispel the tingling in her fingers that she knew was the beginnings of a panic attack.

She'd had a few of them after the breakup with Phillip, wondering whether she'd done the right thing.

Gradually her breathing settled, and she began to feel slightly better.

'Here is the town.' Mistress Oatley pointed, and Beth stood still as she saw the colourful stalls ahead, and the crowds of people jostling to look at the goods on display.

'Oh, my,' she said lifting one hand to her mouth. 'It is nothing like I imagined.'

The opportunity to stay and study a period of history by being a very part of it was tempting. For a moment, Beth put aside her worry of not being able to return through the stones and considered perhaps staying here for a while.

But that would be foolish; it was too much of an unknown.

Would she be able to get back if she stayed longer than a certain time? Maybe Alice had known something and that's why she had left suddenly.

'Remember to stay close by me, and not speak.' Mistress Oatley instructed.

'I will.' She reached up to pull her head piece down a little and her hand shook.

'Are you feeling poorly again? Perhaps you should have stayed at the manor.' Mistress

Oatley's voice was sharp, but her expression was concerned.

'No. I am well. Come, let's go and see what wares are to be had.' Beth smiled; she was getting the hang of this medieval speech. If she was here to stay, she had a lot to learn.

She followed the housekeeper into the surging crowd and watched with interest as the woman haggled for the best price for the colourful dried fruits on display. Beth's fingers itched to take notes, but she had no pen or paper, and her phone hadn't worked since she'd woken up beside the stones.

They were halfway along the first row of stalls when a loud voice rose above the noise of the crowd.

'Mistress Oatley!'

The older woman turned and nodded to Beth to follow her.

'Good morning, Mistress Clifford. Do you have your herb bunches today?'

The other woman nodded but she seemed distracted as she stared at Beth. 'Aye, I do.'

Eventually she turned to the bags of herbs hanging from the side of her tent and clipped two off with a sharp knife. 'The sage has been very good this summer,' she said.

Beth's attention wandered as the two women discussed the merits of various herbs.

Her head was aching slightly, and she was thirsty; she'd kill for a Coke.

There's no chance of getting one of them at a medieval market in Glastonbury.

There was a small wooden stool at the side of the stall, and she walked over and sat down as the two women continued chatting. A couple of times the woman who ran the stall would flick a curious glance her way, but Beth knew she didn't look out of place now that she had the cloak over her clothes. It was hot, and she reached up and pulled the band from her head to ease the ache in her forehead, and her hair tumbled down.

The woman's eyes stayed on her as she leaned over and said something to Mistress Oatley. The housekeeper nodded and then they put their heads together in an intense conversation.

Mistress Oatley eventually came over to where Beth was sitting. 'Are you feeling all right, my dear?'

Beth nodded as she stood again. 'Just a little tired and a headache. Have you finished here?'

'Almost. Mistress Clifford seems to think that your brother is looking for you. I told her that you were a relative of another visitor to the manor, but she wanted me to ask you. She seemed concerned. It is your hair that caught her attention.'

Beth shook her head and smiled. 'I do have a brother. His name is Joshua, but he is a long, long way away from here.'

Mistress Oatley tutted as she placed the two bags of herbs in her basket. 'She has the wrong young woman then. She said his name was Silas.'

Beth gaped at her as her world tilted and stars pricked at her vision. 'Silas?' she said weakly as she grabbed for Mistress Oatley's arm.

'Sit down again, dear. You are very pale, and your skin is clammy. I will go and find you some water.'

'Wait, did you say Silas, or did I mishear?'

Mistress Oatley nodded as the other woman came over. 'Yes, she said Silas. Now hush. Mistress Clifford, the young lady has a headache. Do you have some herbs that I can purchase to ease her aching head? I will go and get some water.' She turned to Beth and put her fingers to her lips, indicating that she not speak. There is a well close by.'

Beth sat there alone as the stall holder went back to the stall, and Mistress Oatley hurried off to find the well.

Silas?

He was here?

Hope began to unfurl in her chest. Of course, if Silas knew about the time travel, and had done it himself, he would have known how to follow her.

But why had it taken him so long? Why wasn't he there when she had woken on the ground last night?

Beth watched as the woman reached down into a bag and pulled out a small brass pot with a stopper of cloth. She walked back over to where Beth was sitting and pulled out the cloth and tipped the pot onto her fingers. The cream was cold as she smeared it on Beth's forehead.

A strong smell of garlic and other herbs tickled Beth's nose, but the smell was not unpleasant.

'What is it?' she asked focusing on keeping the Aussie accent from her words, mindful of Mistress Oatley's instructions.

'It is radish and garlic, with bishop's wort boiled in butter with red nettle. It will ease your aches swiftly.'

Beth nodded but didn't speak.

'I will come back and check on you in a moment. Your headache will ease very quickly.' The woman walked away to attend to a group of customers waiting at her stall.

Mistress Oatley came back with a tankard

of water, and Beth took it from her gratefully.

'Thank you,' she said before she drank deeply of the cold, sweet water.

Instantly, she felt better, and surprisingly the headache had gone too. She stood and handed the tankard back and leaned forward.

'Now tell me about Silas? What did he say? Is he really here?' she whispered.

Mrs Oatley nodded. 'Mistress Clifford said he was most concerned for his sister's wellbeing, as she had run away. Do you know this man? Is he your brother? Should we wait or is his intent of worry to us?

Beth put her hand on the woman's arm. 'If it is Silas, I will be very pleased. And I will leave with him, as he should know how to take me home.'

'Very well. I will wait here with you until he returns.'

##

Silas had walked through every street in the market town and walked through the Abbey, checking the chapel. If Beth was here, he knew she would be fascinated by the history of the abbey and would be sure to want to see the buildings intact in all of its glory. He might not be a history buff, but from the time he'd spent in Glastonbury at the festivals over the years, he knew that in medieval times only Westminster Abbey was more richly endowed and appointed than the abbey at Glastonbury.

He stood and waited his turn at the well as a woman filled a metal tankard with water. The market was even more crowded as the day lengthened. He wondered whether it would go into the night. He was going to have to find somewhere to sleep.

He took his turn at the pump next to the well, and quickly had a drink as the line grew longer behind him. Wiping his face with his wet hands, he headed back to the herb stall to see if the woman had seen any sign of Beth. Silas was and his head still ached slightly. His spirits were low, and he knew he would have to consider going back without Beth. Perhaps he'd not looked closely enough, and he'd miscalculated when he'd marked the stone.

As he approached the stall, the woman who'd been at the pump ahead of him turned and walked between the stall and a tent on the other side.

Mistress Clifford had a crowd at her stall, so he stepped into the shade and waited for her to finish. His gaze went to the woman who had paused between the two stalls and was speaking to another woman.

Silas's heart almost stopped.

His gaze homed in on the glimpse of auburn hair. The woman had her back to him, and her cloak was grey, but the tilt of her head was Beth's. He shook his head but kept his eyes on the back of her head. She was the right height, but the different cloak threw him.

Slowly and carefully, he made his way through the small crowd at the side of the stall.

'Hoy, you, wait your turn.' A hand grabbed at his coat, but Silas stepped past it, his attention on the red-haired woman only yards away from him.

He had almost reached her when she turned, and her beautiful hair tumbled over her shoulders.

Beth looked up at him and Silas reached out for the woman he loved.

Chapter 28

Tears pricked at Beth's eyes as Silas held her close. His heart thudded against her chest, and although he gripped her tightly, she could feel his hands shaking. The relief of seeing him was dizzying, and she clung to him for a moment, absorbing his familiar smell and feel, before she took a step back.

Mrs Oatley raised her eyebrows and gestured towards Silas. 'This is the man you were hoping for?'

'It is.' Beth clutched her hands together as Silas held her gaze. 'I am very pleased to see you, Silas.'

'And I you.' His tone was level, but his eyes were hooded in the shadow of the stall.

'You have a lot to tell me when we go back.' Beth kept her tone even, although her emotions were see-sawing. Part of her wanted to hold him and keep touching him, and have things back to what they were, but her self-preservation kicked in. Silas had lied to her; and he'd taken advantage of her to get into her bed and stupidly she had fallen for it.

And foolishly fallen for him in the process.

When would she ever learn not to give her trust so readily?

She straightened and undid the loop at the collar of the cloak. 'Mistress Oatley, Silas will take me home now.'

The woman nodded her head at Silas but waved a hand to Beth. 'Keep the cloak, dear. You may need it wherever it is you are going. It is an old one of mine. I will not miss it.'

'Thank you.' Beth reached out to the woman and took her hand. 'Thank you so much for looking after me, Mistress Oatley. Would you please thank Lord Branton? I am sorry I could not speak with him more. There is a lot I would have liked to explain to him.'

'Beth, wait. We can't leave yet.' Silas shook his head as she looked back at him.

'Why not?'

'We have to wait for the right time.' He lowered his voice as the stall holder walked over. 'And that is a day away.'

'You found you sister, then?' she said with a smile.

'I did, thank you for passing my message on.'

'Has your headache eased, lass?'

'It has, thank you, but I am sorry,' Beth said. 'I have no money to pay you for your remedy.'

The woman waved a dismissive hand. 'Not to worry. Mistress Oatley spends enough of her master's coin at my market each month.'

'Thank you, Mistress Clifford. We appreciate that.' Mistress Oatley stepped forward and put a hand on Silas's arm. 'Perhaps you would like to come back to the manor with me if you are not leaving Glastonbury now.'

They said goodbye to the herb-seller, and walked along to the edge of the field where the stones sat in brooding silence.

Silas looked at Beth. 'We have to find somewhere to stay tonight.'

'I am sure the master will be pleased to have you stay the night at the manor,' Mistress Oatley said.

'You are the one I have to trust to get me home.' The word was bitter in Beth's mouth. 'But I am sure Lord Branton will let you sleep in a stable or the like if we must wait.' Beth nodded at Silas.

***

Silas knew something was bothering Beth.

He walked behind the two women as they made their way across the fields and up a hill, and then across a smaller field until they reached a honey-coloured brick manor house set in the midst of extensive gardens. He carried the two baskets and the two women chatted together in front of him as though they were lifelong friends.

Beth barely looked back and when they reached the entrance of the house, she finally turned her attention to him.

'When is the right time to leave?' she asked.

Mistress Oatley took the baskets from him and ushered them inside. 'You can sit in the parlour, while I work in the kitchen. I imagine that Lord Branton will be back soon, and you can partake of refreshments with him.' She disappeared down a dim hall and Silas followed Beth through another door.

It was a long narrow room that looked out over the gardens. She pointed to a wooden chair against a wall. 'You sit there.'

Before he could sit down, she removed her coat and sat on a window seat a distance away from the chair. She held her head stiffly, and her lips were set in a straight line.

Silas sat down and looked at her, and a surge of love filled his chest. 'We'll get back, Beth, don't worry.'

'That's good to hear.' She turned her head away from him looked out the window.

'Is your head still aching? It happens to me

too each time.'

'No. I'm fine. 'The voice was still clipped, and she didn't look at him.

'That's good.'

The only sound was a door closing somewhere along the hall, and finally Silas had had enough.

'Beth, is there something bothering you?'

Slowly she turned her head and stared at him, her expression closed. 'Apart from finding myself at the end of the fifteenth century?' Ice almost dripped from her words. 'I'm also angry with myself.'

'It's all right. We'll get back. I know how to get us home, so you can chill.'

She inclined her head in a regal fashion. 'I believe that as well as you knowing all about it, Megan, and David, and Alice, and quite possibly my mother all know about this time stuff.'

Ah, so that was the problem. Silas pushed himself up from the hard chair and crossed to the window seat and sat beside her. He reached out to take her hand, but she snatched it back.

'Don't touch me.'

He pulled his hand back as pure venom laced her tone. His temper began to fire in return. 'I don't know about your mother, but yes, Megan and David and Alice knew about the time slip.'

'And you too, obviously?' she said as she moved along the seat away from him. 'It would have made for interesting entertainment if you'd shared it with me.' Her eyes glittered as they met his. 'But no. Knowing Megan and all the discouragement she gave me about staying there, I'd say that you were put next door to look after me. Do me the courtesy of being honest, Silas. Am I right?'

He held her gaze as he nodded. 'Yes. That's why I was there. To keep you safe.'

Her chin lifted higher. 'And how convenient for you that I fell into your arms at the wedding. A bit of sex on the side would have made the babysitting a less arduous task for you?'

'No, you're wrong there.'

'Oh, don't give me that. I made the mistake of trusting you once, but I won't do it again. I've learned my lesson with Phillip and my father.'

'Beth, don't be ridiculous.' He moved along the seat, but she put her hand up.

'You can try as much as you like to convince me, but I will not fall for it again. Been there, done that. Just get me home and then you can go to wherever it is you live.' Her eyes narrowed. 'Or should it be whenever?'

Silas ran a hand through his hair as frustration took hold. Whatever he said he was going to sound like a lie.

'Okay, the truth. I won't lie to you. I'm from 1971 and so is Davy, but when he fell in love with Megan, he decided to stay here. Or there, I mean. And I've been talking about staying too.'

'I'm not that easy, Silas. So don't get your hopes up.'

'That's not what I meant. I'd already spoken to Davy and Megan about it before I even met you. You can check with them.'

'I'm not interested in anything you have to say. Just take me back.'

He leaned back against the window trying to think of the right words to say, but Beth spoke again before he could. The tremble in her voice broke his heart; all he wanted to do was hold her and comfort her, but as he was the primary cause of her angst, that wasn't going to be welcome.

'Are you sure we can get back? Tell me how it happens.' She turned her head so that she was looking through the window again. 'I've already tried once, and nothing happened.'

'It has to be at noon. The time is critical. Noon or midnight. The destination is determined by where you touch the rock.'

'How do you know where to touch it? What happens if you touch it in the wrong place? Are you saying we could end up in another time?

He nodded, but hurried to reassure her. 'We could, but it's all right. I marked the stone when I arrived. We'll go back to where—when—we came from.' He held her eye as she turned back to him. 'I'm afraid you will have to trust me on that. The only problem we might have is knowing the exact time, but I noticed that the abbey rings bells on the hour every three hours. If we wait there until the sun is high, the humming will tell us when it is close.'

Before Beth could answer, the door opened and a tall man with dark hair strode in. Silas stood as he crossed the room to the window.

Beth jumped to her feet and stood beside him. 'Lord Branton.'

'Mistress Beth.' He nodded and turned to Silas. 'Mistress Oatley told me you are a relative of Beth's and have come to take her home?'

'I am. Thank you for taking care of

her, sir.'

'I believe that you also need lodging tonight before you make your long journey home,' Lord Branton said. 'You are most welcome to stay here.'

Silas started as Beth's hand crept into the crook of his elbow and she pressed a warning.

She spoke before he could answer. 'That is very kind of you. Mistress Oatley told me that you also wished to speak to me?'

The man nodded. 'I wish to hear more of Alice before you take your leave.'

'Silas, I am sure that Lord Branton can find some chores for you while I speak with him. To make payment for our lodgings.'

'That would be most helpful. My men have gone to Exeter to support the king. Come, I will take you to the stables, and show you where you can sleep, and then there are some sheep to be moved. Are you able to help with that?'

'I know sheep,' Silas said gruffly.

He was tempted to pull his forelock, but he made do with a searing glance at Beth as he followed the lord from the room. The hint of a smile on her lips set off a small spark of hope in Silas's chest.

Chapter 29

Being merely a travel companion, Silas was relegated to the stables for his lodging, and to the kitchen for his meal. His curiosity as to what was being spoken of in the parlour and the dining room that night, as Beth dined with Lord Branton, bordered on jealousy.

He also worried that she would say too much about their travel, but then he remembered the gentle pressure of her fingers on the inside of his arm. She may not be able to trust him, but he would trust her.

If there was to be any future together, he could give her his trust.

He woke early the next morning as the bells of the abbey pealed. Mistress Oatley had told him of the liturgy of the bells when they had rung last night as he'd eaten the delicious stew she had served for him.

He'd cocked his head to the side. 'Do the bells ring regularly at the abbey? I am not familiar with it. There is no abbey near where we live.'

'That is vespers at the abbey.' She bustled around the table and put another chunk of warm bread in front of him. 'It is when the monks come to prayer. You will hear compline in another three hours and then matins at midnight, lauds at dawn, prime in the morning and so on.

'Is there a call at noon?' he asked.

'Yes, that is called sext.'

He awoke to bells and assumed that was the prime call and figured that would be six a.m. He wanted to be at the stones as early as they could get there. Not having a working time piece made it hard.

As Silas washed in the tub of water in the stable, the sound of horse's hooves ringing on the cobblestones had him going to the door. The talk of war and uprisings had Silas nervous and he wasn't going to relax for one minute until he had Beth home safely.

It was Lord Branton. Silas watched as he cantered down the long drive and then the horse turned to the north. It was only a few minutes later that Beth appeared in the doorway. She was wearing her coat this time, and she carried a basket.

'Mistress Oatley packed some food for us. She has gone to her sister's for the birth of a child.'

'And Lord Branton?' Silas was stung by the lack of a greeting, or even a "how did you sleep?"'

'He has gone to Exeter to be with his men. I have a bad feeling about it. We said our farewells last night.'

Silas nodded abruptly and reached for his boots. 'So you're ready to go?'

'I am.'

Any hope that the walk to the stones would give him a chance to win Beth's trust faded quickly. They spoke but the conversation was about the time they were in. Silas explained about the abbey bells, but as he should have known, Beth was already familiar with them.

And more.

'The invention of the mechanical clock was one of the most remarkable legacies of the medieval period. I would say that the abbey has a clock. Most towns had at least one by the end of the fifteenth century.'

'Interesting,' Silas said as they reached the top of the hill and looked down at the markers.

'Yes, experiments with gearing systems and weights led to the invention of the foliot escapement and the first mechanical clock appeared probably about two hundred years ago. Late thirteenth century, I mean,' Beth said.

'We take a lot for granted in our time, don't we?' Silas said pulling out his dead phone and staring at it.

'By this time most towns had at least one clock, because they could be used for working hours, especially in towns where there were many craftsmen. It allowed them to charge for their time.'

'How do you know all this? Silas shook his head, but Beth wasn't to be drawn into the personal.

'It's my job.' She looked up at the sky, and a shimmer of nerves seemed to cross her expression.

Silas couldn't help himself. 'Don't worry, Beth. I'll look after you. There is little to be nervous about. Maybe another headache when we get back, but we've keep hydrated so we should be right. Do you want to take that with us?' He gestured to the basket, and the eating implements that Mistress Oatley had packed.

'Not this time. Just let me see that we can get back safely.'

'Not *this* time?' Silas stared at her.

***

Being with Silas, and trying to keep her distance, and remind herself that she could not trust him was one of the hardest things that Beth had ever done. But she stayed strong, and the conversation was impersonal. She probably had sounded like a know-it-all-pain as she delivered lecture after lecture on various aspects of medieval society. At one stage his eyes had glazed over as they'd walked across the field and she'd hidden a grin.

Being here in the fifteenth century was amazing, and Beth realised how much of the history that she had studied was wrong. She had to come back. Once she knew it was safe and possible to travel she would return.

The conversation with Branton last night had been an eye-opener; she'd learned so much about Alice. She'd sensed his frustration when she wouldn't tell him any more than that Alice had passed away. No matter how many times he'd asked—almost begged—what village she had come from, she would not say.

Shaking her head, she had replied. 'If Alice had wanted you to know, she would have told you herself.'

Even though she had told Branton that Alice had passed, she was hopeful that Alice had returned to him at a later time. If Beth couldn't come back here at another time, there were still the parish records, and she could do her research back at Glastonbury.

As much as Beth was cynical about happy endings, she needed to know that there had been one for her great aunt and Branton. As they began the descent to the stones the sound of a horse's hooves reached them from the road below. Branton jumped his horse over the drystone wall and cantered up to them.

'By God, I am pleased to have caught you. Mistress Beth. I need Silas for a while. My men are on the way to Taunton already. Can you spare me a few hours before you begin your journey?'

'What do you need?' Silas's voice held reluctance, but the desperate pleading in Branton's voice was hard to ignore.

'The King's scouts have just left Glastonbury, and I am meeting them at the crossroads eight miles away. The Cornish army is almost to Taunton. Old Sam is a farm horse and will not be able to travel the twenty miles to there.'

'But how will you get there?' Beth asked as her eyes widened and she looked at Silas.

'They have a horse waiting for me. I need you to ride with me and bring Sam back to the stable. Come quickly, we do not have time to tarry.' He reached a hand down to Silas. 'I will pay you well.'

'I don't expect to be paid. Give me one minute.' Silas turned to Beth and took her by the shoulders. 'It's not safe to be by yourself if there are troops about. Go back to the manor and wait for me. If I am not back by the next bells—he lowered his voice—'wait an hour after that and then make your way to the stones. You must be there ready to go for noon. Stay hidden as much as you can when you get there.'

'I won't go without you.'

'I will be back.' Silas took Branton's hand and climbed onto the back of the old horse behind him.

'But remember what I said. An hour after the bells and the mark that I made.'

Branton wheeled the horse around and Silas looked back at her.

'I love you, Beth.'

***

Beth sat in the parlour waiting for the sounds of Silas returning on the horse. If they were traveling eight miles to get there, and then he had eight miles to return, she calculated that it would take two hours to get there, and perhaps a little less to return. Although the horse would be tired after travelling at speed with two grown men on its back, so it could be four hours at least. It had been about seven o'clock when they had set out across the fields, so if all went well, Silas would return about an hour before noon.

The minutes dragged. She was alone in the house; there was no point sitting there waiting; there was no way Silas would be back for at least three hours. Feeling slightly like an intruder, Beth wandered around the house looking at the way a household was run in the fifteenth century. It filled in the time as she looked in the kitchen and the scullery at the back of the house. She walked back through the parlour and into a Great Hall decorated with huge tapestries and ornate lamps on the walls. The rooms were all panelled with dark timber, and the walls in this hall had intricate carvings around the mantlepiece.

Oh, for a camera.

Next time. If there was a next time.

She went outside and looked at the intricate layout of the brick gardens in a herringbone pattern. It amazed her that a manor house of this size had so few staff. She had had so much she wanted to ask Branton last night, but most of their conversation had been about Alice, not about the manor house.

She wished she could ask him all of the questions that were tripping through her head now. At the back of the chapel a small stream ran along the fields and in the distance, Beth could see the water mill. She hurried along the bank and smiled when she reached the huge tree further downstream.

This afternoon we lay under the spreading beech tree down the stream from the watermill, I lay there with my head in Branton's lap reciting my favourite poem.

'While barred clouds bloom the soft-dying day,
And touch the stubble-plains with rosy hue;
 Then in a wailful choir the small gnats mourn.'

She closed her eyes as she remembered Alice's words. This is where Alice had lain with Branton after the harvest. Her throat ached with unshed tears as she thought of lost love; she had seen how much Branton was suffering.

Oh, I do hope Alice came back.

When—if—she got back to the cottage, Beth vowed she would read the journals until she found out the truth.

She made her way slowly back to the house, thinking the more time she took, the more chance there was of Silas being back there. Many men she knew would not have helped so readily, but it was clear that Branton was distressed, and Silas had risked his return to help him. Her last sight of him had been on the back of an old white horse, calling out to her that he loved her.

Maybe she could begin to trust. Maybe he was telling the truth.

As she walked back to the parlour the pealing of the bells at the abbey drifted in through the window and Beth clenched her hands tightly at her sides.

Please be there.

But there was no sign of Silas. She gathered her coat, and the food that Mistress Oatley had packed.

She sat and counted the seconds, the minutes, and waited, but when she reached forty-five minutes after the bells there was still no sound of a horse returning. Going out through the scullery, she detoured via the stables, but they were empty.

Knowing she couldn't dally any longer, Beth walked down the path to the gate, listening for the pounding of hooves.

But there was only silence.

There was no one on the path, and the fields were bare of sheep. It was as though she was the only living creature in the world. A shiver ran down Beth's back as she approached the three stones. The sun was high in the sky and it had to be getting close to eleven. He should be back soon. He had to come back to her.

Silas hadn't had to follow her, but he had, and she'd treated him badly.

Beth sat with her back to the stones and waited.

And waited.

But there was no sign of him. Tears seeped from the corners of her eyes and she closed them as desolation settled in her heart.

Should I go?

Should I stay?

'It's time.' The voice was ragged.

Beth looked up as the deep voice broke into her musing. Joy ran through her as Silas stood in front of her holding his hands out.

'By the skin of my teeth.' His Irish accent was strong as he fought for breath. 'I took the horse back and ran all the way from the stables.'

She took his hand, trying to ignore the warmth that ran up her arm and lodged in her heart.

But Aunt Alice's words filled her thoughts as Silas led her to the biggest marker stone in the centre.

Time is fleeting. Seize each opportunity. Make the most of every minute.

She squeezed his fingers, and as he looked down at her, she saw the love in his eyes.

'Silas?' she said softly. 'Just in case…will you kiss me before we go?'

He held her gaze as she stared back at him. 'On one condition.' His breath was warm against her cheek as he spoke.

'I need to know that you trust me wholeheartedly, Beth. Do you?'

She nodded as love blossomed inside of her. All she was aware of was the love in his eyes, the warmth of his breath on her face and the strength of the arms about her.

'And you need to know that I love you more than life itself.' Silas enfolded her in his arms, and he held her close. His eyes held hers as he lowered his mouth slowly to her face.

'I know. And I love you too, Silas.'

Their lips clung and searched as each of them gave and took. It didn't matter where or when they were, time was suspended for them.

As the bells rang out from the abbey signalling noon, Beth drew back slowly, unwilling to relinquish the magic of that kiss.

Silas held her against him and took her hand in his and placed their hands side by side over the mark on the stone. The vibration beneath their fingers came before the humming started and a small frisson of fear ran through Beth. But Silas turned his head and held her gaze with his and Beth knew everything was going to be all right.

Trust.

It took two.

Epilogue

Silas and Beth spent the first few days after they came home in close company. It was a time for getting to know each other, and for Beth, for deepening her trust.

They had come close to losing each other, both through circumstances and with Beth's hesitancy to trust again.

She told Silas of the difficult relationship with her father, and how she'd let Phillip take over her life.

'He sounds like a proper tool,' Silas said one morning as they lay in her bed. 'No offence meant to you, of course.' He rolled over and tipped her chin up with his finger as he lay above her. 'It's very pleasing to see that your taste in men has improved.'

Beth tickled his stomach and he chuckled; she'd learned about his body over the past few days.

And about his character; he was a good man.

When he'd called Davy to let them know that he and Beth had come home safely, she'd heard the emotion in his voice and knew how close they'd come to being separated for ever.

'Silas?'

'Yes?'

Beth was sorry that she put a frown on his face, as he obviously picked up that she had something on her mind. 'You said that you were thinking about about staying here and not going back to your time. Have you thought about it anymore?'

He sat up and was quiet for a long time. Beth sat up beside him and Silas put his arm around her.

'I have given it a lot of thought, and I have decided.

She held her breath as he seemed to hesitate., and the words rushed out. 'It's okay. I understand if you want to go back. It would be very hard learning to live in a different time.'

Silas shook his head. 'Do you think so? Did you find the time you spent at the manor difficult?'

Beth bit her lip. 'No,' she said slowly. 'It didn't take very long for me to adjust, once I knew where everything was.'

'We depend on a lot of technology that is useful, and makes life easier, but it's not really necessary, is it?'

Beth lifted her head and her heart raced as she spoke of what was on her mind. She had been going to bide her time, but if Silas was thinking about going back to his time, she would be honest. She trusted him. If Silas chose to leave her, it would be very hard, but she would understand why.

He folded her in a close hug and put his lips against her forehead. 'Sweetheart, I'm not going back. I'm here with you to stay, and you're stuck with me.'

'I'm very pleased to hear that.' Relief filled her chest, and Beth lifted her lips to meet his. After a few seconds, she pulled back. 'I want to ask you something.'

'Yes, I do love you.'

She smiled against his lips as he bent to kiss her again. 'I know that already, and I love you.'

'So what's on your mind?'

'Alice,' she said and it was hard to keep sadness from her voice. 'And Branton. I want to know if she went back. I want to go back and find out.'

'Back to their time? Or his time? Who knows when Alice's time really was,' Silas said.

'Yes. Back to when we were.' Beth shook her head. 'I can't believe I'm in bed with you having a conversation about visiting the fifteenth century.'

'I'm very happy with where you are.' His arms tightened about her. 'But if you want to travel again, we'll do it together. But not for a while.'

'I agree. I want to finish reading the diaries, and I want to prepare this time. The historical research I could do there would be amazing if I had a camera that worked.'

'We'll give it some thought. But Beth, we have to be careful. Davy and I have talked about this often. We don't know if our actions there could change the future.'

'I understand what you're saying. And I want to talk to my mother. I have a feeling that she knows a lot more about Alice than she ever admitted to. I always remember Dad saying something about a "missing bloke" and Mum hushing him. I wondered if maybe Branton came back with Alice.'

'After the time we were there?'

'Yes, he was genuinely distressed about her going, so it wasn't before then.' Beth stared at the wall, as she thought of Alice's words. 'There was a child. I think she must have miscarried.'

'Jesus. That's the sort of thing that could change the future. We'll read the diaries, and you can call your mum, and then we'll talk to Davy. Are you happy with that?'

'I am.' Beth snuggled into his bare chest and closed her eyes. She giggled as his stomach grumbled. 'I don't think we had dinner last night, did we?'

'No, you side-tracked me, and dragged me to bed. I'm almost faint with hunger. So, wench, are you going to cook my breakfast?'

Silas climbed out of bed and Beth looked her fill at the man she loved; the man who understood her. He stood beside the bed, letting her gaze trail over the muscular chest, down to that sexy V—

A pounding on the door interrupted her pleasure and she frowned. 'Who on earth could that be?'

Silas grabbed his jeans and put them on and crossed to the window. He opened the window and yelled down. 'The door's unlocked. We'll be down in a minute.' He turned to Beth as he pulled a T-shirt over his chest. 'Looks like we're feeding a few, sweetheart. I recognised Davy and Megan's Land Rover, but I don't know who the woman is getting out of the taxi.'

Beth jumped out of bed and ran for the bathroom. 'You keep them entertained. I'm going to take a shower.'

'Make it quick.' He grabbed her for a slow kiss on the way past. 'I have a feeling there'll be more explaining to do than entertaining.'

Beth hurried in the shower and looked around for something decent to wear. There hadn't been a need for much in the way of clothing over the past few days, and most nights, they'd snuggled up in front of the fire together beneath a blanket, reading Alice's journals. So far, they had learned little that they didn't already know but Beth wasn't going to give up hoping that Alice had gone back to Branton.

She pulled on a pair of leggings and picked up the angora jumper that was on the back of the chair. A cursory brush of her hair, and she looped it up and caught it in a clip, before putting on a smudge of lip gloss. Closing the door quietly, she walked slowly down the stairs. The aroma of freshly-brewed coffee tickled her nose and she smiled. David and Silas were standing by the fire, but there was no sign of Megan.

'Megan made the coffee?' she asked.

Silas nodded but he looked anxious. 'Yes. They're in the kitchen.'

'They?' she said with a quizzical look at Silas.

'Hello, Beth. It's very good to see you.' David dropped a kiss on the top of her head.

'And you, too.' She headed for the kitchen, wondering who was in there, but stopped dead and put a hand to her mouth as the door opened. Megan carried out a tray of coffee and buttered toast, but it was the other woman who held Beth's undivided attention.

'My God, Mum! What are you doing here? I was just talking about you!'

'Hello, darling. It's lovely to see you too.' Her mother's smile was brittle, but sad.

'It's great to see you. I mean it, Mum.' Beth walked into her mother's open arms and hugged her. 'I was just flabbergasted when you walked out of the kitchen. You should have told me you were coming.'

'I think perhaps where you were, it may have been hard to get a message to you.'

Beth's eyes widened as she looked from her mother to Megan.

'Hello, Beth,' Megan said quietly, reaching out and squeezing her fingers.

'What's going on?' Beth looked around, feeling as though she had been left out of the loop again. 'Mum, have you met Silas?'

'I have. Can we sit down and have a coffee before we chat,' her mother said. 'It's a long way from London in a little black taxi.'

Silas must have taken pity on Beth, because he walked over and took her hand. 'Be a love and pour Beth and Lucy a coffee, Megs.' He led Beth to the sofa and sat beside her and put his arm around her shoulders.

Okay, that was the first hurdle over. He'd made a public announcement of their relationship, but no one seemed terribly surprised.

By the time the coffees were poured, and everyone was sitting down, Beth was bemused; she felt as though she had gone down the rabbit hole.

'I want to go first, before we get all serious,' Megan said. 'I didn't tell you at the wedding and then when Silas rang to say you'd disappeared, I thought you'd never know.'

'Never know what?

'That you're going to be a godmother.'

Beth squealed and jumped up to hug Megan. 'That is fabulous, fabulous news.'

'Congratulations, Megan and David. That's wonderful,' Mum said quietly.

'Thanks, Lucy.' Megan hugged her too before she went back across to David.

Beth looked curiously at her mother as she sat in the chair opposite the sofa. Somehow, she seemed softer, and calmer. Her eyes were bright and clear, and her hands were steady.

Beth sat back next to Silas and his arm held her close again. 'Okay, Mum. Now tell me why you're here.'

Her mother looked at her steadily, and Beth was worried when she saw her lips tremble.

'Because I know what can happen here, and when I heard that you had gone—'

'Hang on,' Beth said. 'Does the whole world know about my adventure?'

'No.' Mum shook her head. 'When I arrived, I couldn't get your mobile so I rang Megan to see if you'd stayed up in Scotland after the wedding. I was hoping you had. The further you were away from this cottage the better I would have felt. I interrupted their honeymoon—'

David interrupted. 'No, you didn't. As soon as I took Silas's call, we were on the first plane back here.'

'Why, Mum. How did you know about it?'

'About the stones? Because I've been there.'

Beth's mouth was open, and she shook her head. 'Been where?'

'There is a story I have to tell you.'

'About Alice?'

'No, about me and your father.'

'Dad went too?'

'No, your real father.'

Silas took Beth's hand and held it tightly. Whatever was coming, she had the man she loved by her side. Everything would be all right. What would Alice have said?

Time is fleeting. Seize each opportunity.

Make the most of every minute.

THE END

Next in series: Finding Home

OTHER BOOKS from ANNIE

Whitsunday Dawn
Undara
Osprey Reef
East of Alice

Porter Sisters Series

Kakadu Sunset
Daintree
Diamond Sky
Hidden Valley
Larapinta
Kakadu Dawn

Pentecost Island Series

Pippa
Eliza
Nell
Tamsin
Evie
Cherry
Odessa
Sienna
Tess
Isla

The Augathella Girls Series
Outback Roads
Outback Sky
Outback Escape
Outback Wind
Outback Dawn
Outback Moonlight
Outback Dust
Outback Hope
An Augathella Surprise
An Augathella Baby
An Augathella Spring

Sunshine Coast Series
Waiting for Ana
The Trouble with Jack
Healing His Heart
Sunshine Coast Boxed Set

The Richards Brothers Series
The Trouble with Paradise
Marry in Haste
Outback Sunrise
Richards Brothers Boxed Set

Bondi Beach Love Series
Beach House
Beach Music
Beach Walk
Beach Dreams
The House on the Hill

Second Chance Bay Series
Her Outback Playboy

ANNIE SEATON

Her Outback Protector
Her Outback Haven
Her Outback Paradise
The McDougalls of Second Chance Bay Boxed Set

Love Across Time Series
Come Back to Me
Follow Me
Finding Home
The Threads that Bind
Love Across Time 1-4 Boxed Set

Bindarra Creek
Worth the Wait
Full Circle
Secrets of River Cottage
A Clever Christmas
A Place to Belong

Four Seasons Short and Sweet
Ten Days in Paradise
Follow the Sun

Others
Deadly Secrets
Adventures in Time
Silver Valley Witch
The Emerald Necklace
Christmas with the Boss
Her Christmas Star
An Aussie Christmas Duo (two Christmas novellas)

About the Author

2023: Winner of the long contemporary RUBY award for *Larapinta*

Finalist for the NZ KORU award 2018 and 2020.

Winner ...Best Established Author of the Year 2017 AUSROM

Long listed for the Sisters in Crime Davitt Awards 2016, 2017, 2018, 2019

Finalist in Book of the Year, Long Romance, RWA Ruby Awards 2016 *Kakadu Sunset*

Winner ...Best Established Author of the Year 2015 AUSROM

Winner ...Author of the Year 2014 AUSROM
Best Established Author, Ausrom Readers' Choice 2017
Book of the Year (Whitsunday Dawn) Ausrom Readers' Choice Awards 2018

Annie lives in Australia, on the beautiful north coast of New South Wales. She sits in her writing chair and looks out over the tranquil Pacific Ocean. She has fulfilled her lifelong dream of becoming an author, and is producing books at a prolific rate.

She writes contemporary romance and loves telling the stories that always have a happily ever after. She lives with her very own hero of many years and they share their home with Toby, the naughtiest dog in the universe, and Barney, the rag doll kitten, who hides when the grandchildren come to visit.

Stay up to date with her latest releases at her website: http://www.annieseaton.net

If you would like to stay up to date with Annie's releases, subscribe to her newsletter on her website.

FOLLOW ME

www.ingramcontent.com/pod-product-compliance
Lightning Source LLC
Chambersburg PA
CBHW021422110726
47901CB00008B/2259